DANNY ORLIS

AND

DEEDEE'S DEFIANCE

DANNY ORLIS

AND

DEEDEE'S DEFIANCE

BERNARD PALMER

Please note that several books in the Danny Orlis series are published by Sword of the Lord Publications and are available for purchase on their website, www.swordbooks.com.

Aneko Press *Youth*

www.anekopress.com

Aneko Press, Life Sentence Publishing, and our logos are trademarks of Life Sentence Publishing, Inc.
203 E. Birch Street
P.O. Box 652
Abbotsford, WI 54405

JUVENILE FICTION / Religious / Christian / Action & Adventure
Paperback ISBN: 979-8-88936-058-2
eBook ISBN: 979-8-88936-059-9
10 9 8 7 6 5 4 3 2 1
Available where books are sold

CONTENTS

CHAPTER 1

THE CROW TRAP

The wind howled out of the north, ripping across the scrub timber that surrounded the Orlis farm home and choking the road with drifting snow. The hard winter had caused the deer to leave the woods and seek the farmers' haystacks for something to eat. Rabbits had stripped bark from the trees, as high as they could reach, and the foxes ranged far from their lairs, looking for something to fill their stomachs.

Del Davis was concerned about Jumper, his pet deer, but he knew that Jumper had learned to take care of himself. Blackie, the crow that had stayed behind when the flocks headed south, was foremost in his mind now. Del scrambled out of bed, fearfully got into his clothes, and dashed into the living room to the frost-crusted window where he stared across the bleak, snow-covered farmyard for some sign of the crow.

Danny Orlis saw his concern and knew the cause of it. He had been watching him do the same thing each morning for the last three weeks.

"You don't have to worry about that crow taking off now, Del," he said. "That old boy's too smart to fly south and leave his meal ticket. He knows when he's got a good thing going. He's going to stay around here and eat just as long as you feed him."

Del had heard that before, and it was comforting, he had to admit. He wished he knew half as much about the animals and birds of the North as Danny did. But it did not entirely remove his fear.

"I still keep thinking he might get shot or hurt, or that he just might get tired of staying around here and go somewhere else."

By that time Doug had dressed and came into the living room, buttoning his shirt. "Don't tell me you're still worried about that stupid crow!" Disdain edged his voice as he teased his brother.

"You'll change your tune when I catch him and teach him to talk."

"Catch him? Hah! You'll never be able to lay a hand on that crow. You just wait and see! Crows are smart!"

Del had found himself thinking the same thing from time to time, but he didn't dare to let Doug know that he had any doubts about his ability to catch Blackie. Doug was so sure he couldn't. He had to show him!

Del had talked with Barney Aubichon at length about catching the crow. Barney was a Cree Indian from Canada who was living in a cabin by the lake near the Orlis farm. He knew all about such things and had told Del how to get Blackie to feed in the same place every day in order to get him used to going there. It couldn't be just any place; it had to be the crotch of a tree.

Barney had told him he had a scheme that would catch the crow once Del succeeded in breaking down Blackie's natural wariness, but he didn't go into detail. Del wondered what the rest of the plan was, but he knew better than to ask Barney. He would find out when the time came, and not before.

Every morning before going to school Del took some grain or suet out to the crotch of a tree where he had wedged a small can. After a week or so the wily crow learned that he had nothing to fear from Del. He watched for him and as soon as he left, the bird would come swooping in to feed. Del began to think about going out to see Barney to find out what else he should do in order to catch Blackie.

On Saturday morning he saddled his horse and rode out to the old Indian's log cabin.

Barney was waiting for him, a warm smile on his broad face. "I suppose you think you have that crow of yours trained to eat out of the crotch of the tree, eh?"

Del nodded. "He comes swooping right in just as soon as I leave. I'm ready to catch him now, Barney."

Barney motioned him into the cabin and had him sit down at the table near the little window.

"You think you have Mr. Crow tamed now, eh?" He was chuckling quietly as he lowered himself into the chair across from his youthful visitor.

"He's so tame now I could almost catch him with my hands."

Barney's dark eyes danced. "You try it, my young friend, and you will find out Mr. Crow is not so tame as you think he is. You have to feed him for another week or two, maybe. Then we talk about what to do next."

Del tried to conceal his disappointment and changed the subject.

It was not for another two Saturdays that Barney Aubichon would outline the rest of the plan to him. When Barney did tell him, it came about so casually that at first, he scarcely realized what was happening.

"Have you got an old fishnet around the house?" he asked suddenly.

Del frowned, thinking. Seines were illegal. And besides, Danny wouldn't have one anyway. He enjoyed fishing with a hook and line too much for that.

"I don't think we have," he replied, "except an old minnow seine we used to use."

Barney shuffled to the stove, poured some boiling water into the teapot, and brought it back to the table.

"A seine for minnows isn't so very strong, but it will hold your Mr. Crow, I think."

He sat down heavily and pushed his Bible to one side. Using his hands to explain by gesture, the Indian described the method for netting the crow. A piece of minnow seine, three feet square, was to be tied in place above the crotch of the tree where Del had been placing the food.

"Be sure to tie the sides all around," he repeated, "about so far out from the tree crotch." He indicated a distance of a foot or so with his hands. "Then bring it down so the bottom edges are about six or eight inches above the food."

Del noted the directions carefully, but he doubted that the plan would work. "Will the crow go under a net like that?"

Barney nodded. "He will go under it if he has gone there often enough to feel sure there is no danger for him in going to the tree to eat. That is why we could not hurry it. But now I think he is ready. He flies under the net and eats the same as always. Then, when he has finished, he tries to fly away, but pouf! He gets caught in the net, and you have yourself a crow."

Del hesitated. "You're sure it will work?"

"You try it," Barney told him, winking broadly. "Then you come and tell me if it works."

The boy went back home and began to look for the minnow seine. He thought he knew exactly where it was, but he could not find it. He went to Kay and asked her as soon as she came home.

"You'll have to wait until Danny gets back," she said. "I don't have any idea what he did with it."

Doug came into the kitchen where Del and Kay were talking. "Are you figuring on using a minnow seine to catch that stupid crow?"

"That's right." Del's voice was clipped.

His brother laughed. "That's the most ridiculous thing I ever heard of." He went back to the living room, still chuckling.

Del didn't reply, but his temper surged. That Doug thought he was so smart! He'd show him! And then would he ever have the last laugh on him!

It was Monday when Danny got home from his trip north so Del could get him to find the minnow seine for him.

"It's out in the garage, Del," he said. "Don't you remember helping me put it up on the shelf when we finished with it last fall?" He paused curiously. "What do you figure on doing with a minnow net this time of year?"

Del told him about the trap.

"I'd like to cut a piece off the end of the net, if you don't care."

Danny got his jacket. "I'll go out with you and have a look at it. As I remember, it isn't much good."

There were several large holes in the minnow seine. Danny looked it over and tossed it to Del.

"I don't think we can use it for another season. You'd just as well catch your crow with it."

Del wanted to get the trap set right away, but there were some tests coming up at school and he had to spend the evenings studying. It was not until the tests were finished on Friday that he was able to take time to make the trap to catch Blackie.

He climbed the tree and tied a portion of the net securely over the crotch where he had been feeding the crow. When that was done, he baited the trap with oats and a choice piece of suet.

"There," he said to himself as he climbed down. "That should bring the wily old rascal if anything will."

In the house again, Del stood by the kitchen window and looked out toward the trap. Doubts filled his mind. Maybe Blackie had finally pulled out. Maybe he had decided to go somewhere else for a while. He thought about all of the things he had heard about crows – how they seemed to sense when there was danger. He might not come back again.

Del was still standing there when Doug came home after basketball practice. His brother noticed the trap as soon as he came into the yard.

"Caught him yet?" he sang out as he threw open the back door.

Del scowled. "You saw the trap, didn't you?"

"I thought maybe you'd already caught one crow and had put it up to get another one."

"Very funny!"

The crow did not go to the tree during the night, but the next morning shortly after daybreak there was a terrible racket that wakened everybody in the house.

Instantly Del was out of bed. "I've caught him! I've caught him!"

Doug groaned sleepily. "I don't know which is worse, listening to you or that hideous racket outside."

But Del scarcely heard him. He was getting dressed, hurriedly, his fingers fumbling with the buttons on his shirt. He had caught Blackie! He had caught him just as Barney said he would! That old Indian really knew what he was doing when it came to animals and birds. Del decided his friend must be the smartest guy in the whole world when it came to the wildlife of the North.

Del pulled on his shoes and dashed for the door. He had caught his crow! Now let Doug spout off about how dumb he was to try to catch a crow alive. Let Doug talk all he wanted to about how ignorant he was in wanting to have a crow to tame and teach to talk! He guessed he had showed him, all right!

Del was so excited about catching Blackie that he could scarcely wait to get out to the tree where he had set his trap, but he managed to restrain himself and approached slowly. He had learned that from Barney and from his own association with wild birds and animals. Move slowly and calmly so he would not excite the crow more than he was excited already.

As he came close he saw that the trap had worked exactly the way Barney said that it would. The crow was so entangled in the net he could not free himself. And he didn't like it. He was scolding the world in wild, discordant tones.

"There now, Blackie," Del said, grasping the bird gently. With care he began to cut him out of the minnow seine. "You don't need to get so shaken up. I'm not going to hurt you."

The crow's noisy indignation gave way to fear as Del took hold of him. All was silent.

"Take it easy, old boy," Del went on. "I'll have you out of this mess in no time. I don't blame you for not liking it." He spoke soothingly to the bird as he worked.

By the time Del got back in the house with the bird, everyone was up.

DeeDee pulled her bright colored housecoat closely about herself as she moved near, looking curiously at the bird. Although she wouldn't let Del know it, she was a little afraid. "Have you got a cage fixed for him?"

Del nodded. "Sort of. But it's not a very good one. I thought I'd better wait until I saw whether we caught him or not."

Kay reached out to touch the bird on the head with the tip of her finger. "You aren't going to keep him in a cage, are you?" The tone in her voice revealed what she thought of that.

Danny was the one who answered. "If he's like the crow I used to have, you'll only need a cage for a little while. After he's learned that you're not going to hurt him and that he's going to be fed regularly, you can let him go free. You won't be able to drive him away."

As soon as breakfast was over, Del saddled his horse and took Blackie in the cage over to Barney Aubichon's.

Barney was as excited about it as Del was. "I was sure you'd get him. A trap like that nearly always works."

Del set the cage on the table and pulled out a chair. "I guess I figured we'd get him, too. Only, now that we've got him, I've been wondering what to do next. How are we going about teaching him to talk?"

Barney sat down near the table. "You can't do anything with the crow until you get him tamed, Del. He's got to find out that he can trust you to be kind and not to hurt him. So, that's the first order of business."

"I've already started that. But I keep wondering how I'm going to be able to teach him to talk. Will you help me, Barney?"

The graying Indian chuckled softly. "Now, that's one thing I've never done. But if you want me to, I guess I can try. I tell you what, Del. You leave this guy with me, and I'll teach him to speak Cree!"

CHAPTER 2

SANDY COMES TO VISIT

Two weeks later Sandy Cole came out to the Orlis home to spend Friday night and most of Saturday with DeeDee. This was the first time she had accepted DeeDee's repeated invitation, and she was somewhat uneasy about her stay at the Orlis home. Not that they hadn't made her welcome. She had never been anywhere else where she had felt more at home. The whole family was doing all they could to include her in the things they did.

Everyone, that was, except Doug. And she guessed that was why she wasn't enjoying her stay as much as she had hoped she would. He certainly wasn't around very much. He had some studying to do Friday night, or at least that's what he said. He could hardly take time to eat dinner before hurrying back to his room.

"What's the deal?" Del had wanted to know. "I thought you had all your lessons done for Monday."

Doug's cheeks colored. "I–I've got to do a lot of checking. I'm afraid I missed some answers."

"Maybe I could help you," Sandy had suggested.

The color leaped higher in Doug's face. "Oh, no! I wouldn't think of that. I wouldn't want to spoil your time out here by having you help me."

"That wouldn't spoil anything," Sandy said; but before she finished, Doug had fled. She didn't see any more of him that evening.

The next morning Sandy was determined to spend more time with Doug. She even offered to help when the triplets went to the barn to care for their horses. When DeeDee suggested that she take a ride bareback around the corral, Sandy hesitated. Actually, she was frightened of the western saddle ponies.

"I've never ridden a horse before–." She faltered, then added brightly, "Doug, maybe you could teach me."

Doug turned suddenly and grabbed his saddle off the bench. "Sorry, but my horse needs exercise," he mumbled. "Don't bother to wait around. We'll be gone quite a while."

Later, when Doug returned from his ride, he spent a lot of time helping Del with the crow he had caught a couple of weeks before. Del kept protesting that Doug didn't know anything about Blackie and he wished he'd go on and leave them alone, but Doug pretended he didn't even hear him.

Shortly after lunch Del saddled his horse and

took the crow with him to visit his Indian friend. Sandy thought that surely she and DeeDee would get to be with Doug a little while then. But he went into the kitchen and talked with Danny so softly no one else could hear. The next thing she knew the two of them were going off to the airport. It was almost dinnertime before they came back.

"Is Doug *always* so busy and gone so much?" she asked DeeDee, trying to sound casual about it.

Her friend shrugged. "I don't pay much attention to him, except at mealtimes. He's always here then."

Sandy hesitated. "I thought maybe he would be around more, that's all."

"I'm glad he wasn't. He and Del are both big bores if you ask me." She changed the subject, and Sandy couldn't find out any more about Doug without making it obvious that she was more interested in him than DeeDee thought.

But, aside from not getting to see much of Doug, being at the Orlis home with DeeDee and Danny and Kay had been more fun than Sandy had expected. They laughed a lot, played games, and had a good time.

It seemed that Danny and Kay were really interested in what the triplets liked to do and had time to talk with them about plans and problems. It was a lot different at her house. Her parents were gone so much of the time. She was sorry when the time came to leave the Orlis home.

* * *

Her mother was sitting in the living room alone when Sandy came home.

"Oh, it's you, Sandy," her mother said, looking up as she came in. "Did you have a good time?"

She set her overnight bag in the hall and slipped out of her coat.

"Oh, Mother, it was the most fun!" Before she realized what she was doing, she launched into a detailed description of Danny and Kay's home. "Their place looks so–so comfortable and inviting. You get the feeling that even the house is happy."

A strange, wistful gleam flickered in her eyes.

"Oh, you'd love it, Mother. And you'd love Kay Orlis, too. She's the sweetest person! And she's so much fun!"

"You make her sound like someone very special."

"She is." There was a long silence before Sandy continued. "You know, they're different than we are."

Mrs. Cole eyed her narrowly. Her displeasure at being unfavorably compared with anyone showed through. "In what way?" she asked stiffly.

"Well, after dinner Danny got everyone in the living room and read to them from the Bible. And then he asked if anyone had special things to pray about. DeeDee asked for prayer about her lessons, and Danny wanted them to pray about the trip he was going to be making the first of the week, and Del asked them to pray that he and this Barney person would be able to get his crow, Blackie, to talk."

"That seems like a strange assortment of things to pray about," Mrs. Cole observed. "I can't imagine bothering God with minor things like that."

"It seemed funny to me, too," Sandy went on, "but when they began to pray, I felt different about it. It isn't the kind of praying we do at our church."

"What do you mean by that?"

"It's more like talking to God." She took a deep breath. "As I listened to them, it made me wish that I knew how to pray, Mother."

Mrs. Cole got to her feet after a minute or two and walked to the fireplace where she stood for a long while staring into the fire. At first Sandy thought she must be mad about something, but then she saw that there were tears in her mother's eyes.

* * *

On Monday morning, when DeeDee met Sandy at school, her friend was still thinking about her stay at the Orlis home. All through lunch in the cafeteria she talked about her time at Danny and Kay's.

"They're the nicest people I've ever met," she said. "As long as you can't be with your real parents, you're lucky to be with someone like them."

"Danny and Kay say it wasn't luck. They say that God gave us to them."

Sandy eyed her quizzically. This sort of talk she did not understand. "When I got home Saturday, I was telling Mother all about the place where you live."

DeeDee's smile faded. "The furniture we have is sort of old and dilapidated compared to yours."

Sandy shrugged indifferently. "We've got nice things and the rooms look as though they came from the pages of a magazine, but your place is so comfortable and lived in. It's so homey and inviting." She sighed wistfully. "When I was there, I felt as though I wanted to pull a chair up by the window and curl up in it and do nothing but look out over the lake."

DeeDee completely forgot all the times she had been ashamed of the furniture. She knew what Sandy was talking about. She had felt the same way.

"In the evening we have our devotions in the living room so we can look out over the lake and enjoy the beautiful things God has made for us."

DeeDee hadn't intended to mention their devotions. She knew Sandy didn't go to church very often, and she was afraid of embarrassing her. But it had slipped out.

It didn't seem to bother Sandy, however. She talked about it, openly curious.

"Do you always do that?" she asked. "Do you always read the Bible and pray about things the way you did when I was there?"

DeeDee nodded. "Danny wouldn't miss. And when he's away, Kay does it."

The other girl eyed her wistfully. "I wish we had devotions, or whatever you call it, every night."

DeeDee stared at her. She hadn't expected anything like that from Sandy.

"Maybe you'd like to go to Sunday school and church with me sometime." She spoke timidly, as though still afraid of her friend's reaction.

"I'd love to!"

* * *

Several weeks passed. Del continued working patiently with his crow, Blackie. At first the bird was frightened and would seem to cringe in his cage every time Del approached. For a time, he didn't eat. But Del would talk soothingly to Blackie, reaching through the cage and smoothing his feathers with his fingers. At first Blackie pecked at them, drawing blood a couple of times. But as the days went by and Del continued to work with the crow, Blackie gradually lost his fear. It wasn't long until Del could take him out of his cage for brief periods.

Doug watched the procedure with obvious amusement. "Have you got him talking yet, Del?"

"Just you wait. I'll get him talking." Del spoke with a confidence he did not feel.

"Maybe he'll teach you to talk 'crow' first. Did you ever think of that?"

"Very funny."

"I thought so." Doug was grinning impishly.

Nevertheless, Del continued to work with Blackie. There was only one way to teach a bird like Blackie to talk. That was by repetition, going over the word or phrase again and again until the natural instinct to mimic was aroused.

It wasn't long until Blackie was so tame that he would perch on Del's hand without making an attempt to get away. It seemed to Del that he made more progress after that. Not that Blackie started to talk or anything like that. He had to measure the progress in other ways, in how intently the crow was listening and his feeble attempts to mimic the timbre in Del's voice.

Del spent endless hours working with the crow, repeating the words slowly, time after time after time. And at regular intervals he took Blackie along when he went out to see Barney Aubichon. It soon became the accepted thing for him to go out to the Indian's cabin every Saturday morning.

Barney always expected him, coming to the door as he rode up and inviting him in with a broad grin.

"Come on in and have some cookies and chocolate milk with me, Del. I was just getting ready to have a little lunch."

The boy swung off the saddle horse and handed Barney the cage. "Sounds great. I'll be with you as soon as I get my horse tied."

He slipped the bridle off his saddle pony and put

the halter on. Once inside, he and the elderly Indian set to work, patiently.

"Hello, Blackie," Del began. "Hello. Hello. Hello."

Blackie cocked his head and stared at the boy as though he understood everything that was said to him.

Del continued to repeat the word. "Hello. Hello. Hello."

Barney leaned back in his chair, chuckling silently.

Del glanced up at him. "What's so funny?" he wanted to know.

Barney gradually stopped laughing and wiped at his eyes with the corner of a colored handkerchief.

"I was just wondering what people would think if they'd come along about now and see you trying to talk to a crow."

Del grinned. "They'd probably think I'm crazy." He paused for a moment or two. "And to tell you the truth, Barney, I'm beginning to think the same thing myself. I'm beginning to wonder if we're ever going to be able to get Blackie to say a word."

Barney got ponderously to his feet and shuffled over to the small heater to fill it with wood.

"Are you sure there isn't an easier way to get him to talk than this?" Del persisted.

The elderly Indian shook his head. "There aren't any shortcuts that I know of. A crow can't think the way we do, so the only way he can learn is to hear it often enough until he tries to copy what he hears."

Discouragement clouded Del's eyes. "You mean

I'm going to have to keep this up all the time, if I want him to talk?"

"After a while he'll learn to say the words you've taught him, or those he hears often enough to memorize. Then he'll start talking, and you won't be able to get him to shut up."

Del sighed. "I hope that's right, but I'm beginning to wonder if it's ever going to happen." He turned back to his pet crow. "Hello. Hello." He kept at it tirelessly.

At last, he leaned back in the chair and sighed wearily. "It's no use, Barney. Blackie's too dumb to learn or I'm too dumb to teach him. He's never going to learn to talk."

"Now, wait a minute," Barney countered. "When you and I learned to talk, we didn't get it right off, either. We've been working with Blackie for only a couple of months. We can't give up on him yet."

"Maybe you can't, but I'm ready to quit and turn him loose."

"We're not going to quit after we've worked this long," Barney said firmly. "You just wait. We'll have him speaking before we're through."

At that instant, the crow perked up, as though he suddenly understood everything that was being said. He cocked his head to one side and fixed his gaze on Del Davis.

"'Elio!" Blackie croaked.

Del's eyes widened. The word wasn't too plain, but he could make it out.

"Barney! Did you hear that? Hello. Hello."

Blackie tried again. It was no better than his first effort, but both Del and Barney were listening intently. This time there was no doubt about it. Blackie had spoken.

"'Elio!"

Del jumped to his feet. "We've done it, Barney! We've done it! We've finally got Blackie talking."

CHAPTER 3

BLACKIE'S FIRST WORD

Barney was as excited over the fact that Blackie had finally said a word as Del was, but the Indian remained calm outwardly. He leaned forward intently, black eyes shining.

"Here, let me try." Lips close to the cage, he spoke softly, "Hello, Blackie. Hello. Hello."

Del wasn't sure whether it was his imagination or not, but it seemed to him that Blackie was suddenly paying more attention to them than he had previously when they talked to him. It was almost as though he understood what they were saying to him.

At last Blackie tried once more, mimicking Barney's tone. The word wasn't entirely clear, but it was distinct enough for them to recognize it. There was no doubt about it now. Blackie was starting to talk.

"'Elio. 'Elio."

Barney grinned broadly. "Hear that? That was

plain enough for anyone to understand. I knew he'd get it if we kept working with him long enough."

After that Del took over. He repeated the word slowly, distinctly, giving Blackie time enough to try to speak if he was going to. Once or twice Blackie tried again. Then he lost interest. No matter how hard Del tried, the young crow sulked in his cage and said nothing.

"He won't do it anymore," Del murmured disappointedly.

"I think he's trying to tell you that he's had enough lessons for today and he's going to quit now. But don't you worry, Del. He'll learn fast once he's started to speak. He's one smart crow."

Del leaned back in the chair, excitement dancing in his eyes again. "This is going to be great, Barney." His smile widened. "I can hardly wait until I get back home and show Danny and the others what Blackie can do."

"I'd like to be there when they hear him," Barney murmured. "I can see the look on their faces now."

"Why don't you go back with me, Barney? We can ride double."

Barney looked down at his large stomach and patted it good-naturedly. "You ask me to ride double with you, Del, but your pony would have to do all the work. If he could talk, he would say, 'No, Barney! Please!' "

Del thought for a moment. "You could ride and I could walk."

Barney shook his head. "Some other time I'll go to your house. After Blackie learns to talk better, I'll go and see what they think about it. OK?"

"Oh, sure. Only I hate to have you miss all the fun. You've had more to do with catching Blackie and teaching him to talk than I have."

"I wouldn't say that, Del. I only help what I can. But you can tell me about it the next time you come, eh?"

They sat at the table in the little log shack for an hour or more, talking over their plans for Blackie. They decided what words they were going to teach him and some of the things they would do with him when he could talk clearly enough to be understood by everyone. Then, as usual, they had a short Bible study. Their favorite subject now was birds of the Bible. At last, the time came for Del to go back home.

Barney went out to his pony with him, holding Blackie's cage while Del put the bridle back on his horse and untied the halter rope.

"Don't forget to keep working with him, Del. That's the important thing. Give him his lesson every day. And be sure you stick with one word at a time. Teach him to say hello real good before you try to make him say anything else."

At the sound of the word Blackie's head came up. "'Elio. 'Elio."

"Like I told you," Barney went on, "that Blackie is one smart crow."

Del rode along the lakeshore at a brisk trot. He was more than halfway home when he saw his pet deer standing spraddle-legged in the snow a few yards off the trail. He reined up.

"Hello there, Jumper," he said quietly.

At the sound of the familiar, friendly voice the deer took a step or two toward him. He was timid and a little afraid, but he seemed to remember Del and knew that no harm would come to him through Del.

"Take it easy, pal. There's going to be plenty for you to eat before long. You'll be able to put some meat on those ribs soon."

The deer eyed him curiously but came no closer. Del would have liked to stay there for a time, but he glanced at his watch. He was already almost an hour later than he was supposed to be.

"Sorry, old boy, but Blackie and I've got to beat it or we'll be in big trouble." He lifted the reins. "Besides, we've got some things to show them at the house, haven't we, Blackie?"

With that he clucked to his saddle horse and rode on at a brisk trot. At the first move of the horse, Jumper whirled and dashed into the brush.

Kay and DeeDee were cleaning the dining room when he came bursting in.

"Guess what?" he exclaimed, so excited his voice broke.

His sister glared at him. "Del! You're tracking snow and mud into the house, and we just finished vacuuming the rug!"

He scarcely heard her. "It's finally happened! Blackie can talk! Blackie can talk!"

Kay came over to where he was standing and looked at the floor. She, too, was more interested in the mud he had tracked in than in what he was saying.

"Look at your feet, Del. Why don't you wipe your shoes on that little rug by the door?"

He backed up a few feet and began to wipe his shoes on the rug Kay kept close to the door for that purpose. As he did so, he grumbled under his breath, "Boy, that's something. Here a guy comes home all excited about telling everyone that his crow can talk, and what do they do to him? 'You're tracking the floor!' "

"Well, you were!" DeeDee spoke brusquely. "Just look at the footprints you left on our clean rug!"

He finished wiping his feet before he spoke again. "Just for that, I don't know whether I'll have Blackie talk for you or not. I just might keep him all to myself."

By this time Kay and DeeDee were aware of what Del was trying to tell them. They both turned to him quickly.

"Do you mean he can really and truly talk?" DeeDee demanded.

Del carried Blackie into the kitchen and set the cage on the table. Kay and DeeDee were close behind.

"That's right. He can talk. Over at Barney's he said hello just as plain as anything."

"You're kidding."

Del eyed DeeDee triumphantly. "Now you sound just like Doug. But I'm giving you the straight goods. Blackie can talk!"

DeeDee moved closer, staring incredulously at her brother's crow. It was obvious that she still doubted what Del said. "Would he speak for me?"

"I don't know," Del told her, pride creeping into his voice. "But I think it would be best if you wait until he's trained a little better. Barney says I've got to keep working with him now so he'll really know how to say hello."

Kay spoke up. "Are you going to show us, or are you going to let us die of suspense, Del?"

He pulled up a chair and sat down close to the table where he had put the cage.

"Blackie. Blackie."

The crow's head came up and cocked to one side, saucily.

"Hello. Hello."

There was no answer.

"Blackie!" Del's voice raised imperiously. "Blackie! Hello!"

The crow stared at him but remained mute. Del continued to try to get him to speak; but the harder he tried, the more stupid both he and Blackie appeared.

Kay Orlis was smiling. "I believe he must have forgotten how."

"Or, maybe it was just your imagination." DeeDee's eyes danced gleefully. She could not resist taunting her brother. "Are you sure it wasn't Barney who said hello?"

Del bristled and color tinged his cheeks. "Of course it wasn't Barney!" he snorted indignantly. "I tell you, Blackie talked when we were over there. He talked, and I can prove it."

"Sure you can prove it." DeeDee grinned. "All you've got to do is make him talk now, so we can hear him."

Del got to his feet and picked up the cage.

"Just for that," he exploded. "I won't let you hear him at all. I won't let either of you hear him."

He took the crow out to the little shed where he kept him, slamming the kitchen door behind him as he went.

While he was gone, Danny came in.

"I thought I saw Del in here a little while ago," he said. "What happened to him?"

DeeDee was still smiling. "He came in just a little while ago and tried to tell us that Blackie was talking; but when we asked for a demonstration, he couldn't get him to say a word!"

"I'm afraid we gave him a bad time, Danny. We teased him a little when he couldn't get Blackie to say hello."

Danny pulled out a chair and sat down.

"I remember when Dad and I taught our Blackie to talk. We had the same trouble for a long time. Even after he got to the place where he could say a few words, he would go for days without speaking at all – and that was especially true if there were any strangers around."

"But we're not strangers," DeeDee protested.

"You're not strangers around here," Danny told her. "But as far as Blackie is concerned, you're strangers. He hasn't been around you very much. Unless I'm badly mistaken, it'll be some time before Del will be able to show off his crow's new talents."

"Maybe you'd better go out and tell that to Del," Kay said. "He was feeling terribly deflated when he left the house a little while ago."

* * *

At Minnesota University, Robin and Alex Smith were living in a small apartment just off campus. It was smaller and even more poorly furnished than their first place in Fairview where they lived after getting married while they were still in high school. But it met their need at a low rent, and they were glad for that. Not having a car or a TV didn't bother them particularly, either. They had long since learned to get along on what they had. Besides, all the young couples they knew at school were in the same financial situation. The wives worked while the husbands went to school. And, unless they were getting help from home, the chances were that the husbands tried to hold down at least a part-time job to help meet the bills. That was the way it was with Robin and Alex.

She was working in a discount store as a clerk. She had tried to get a better job; but with her lack of training and experience, that was all that was open, except going to work in a factory on an assembly line and she didn't think she could take such a monotonous job. Alex was carrying a full schedule of classes and working as a night watchman as well.

Having to work this way didn't give them much time to be together, but that was one of the sacrifices that had to be made. Robin was reconciled to that. It wouldn't be too much longer until Alex would graduate and he could get a coaching job somewhere in the state. Then she wouldn't have to work.

Robin was vaguely disturbed that morning as she read the weekly letter from her mother. Things were the same as ever in Fairview. They had been out to Danny and Kay's for coffee after church the week before and had met a young missionary couple who were on their way to Venezuela.

"You write so little about what you and Alex do," her mother wrote in one place. "Where do you go to church? Will Alex go with you?"

Robin's hand trembled as she held the letter. She couldn't remember the last time that her youthful husband had gone to church with her. Not since Christmas the year before, as nearly as she could remember. Actually, she had gotten out of the habit a bit herself, and that wasn't good.

For a long while she sat motionless in the living room, staring at the faded carpet. She was going to have to work on Alex to get him to church again; but she would pray first, asking God to prepare his heart.

CHAPTER 4

DEADLOCKED

Doug Davis and Larry Larson were very disappointed when the basketball season was over and they had to turn in their suits.

"I don't see why we can't keep on playing basketball all spring," Doug said. "Everybody likes basketball a lot better than track or baseball."

"You're sure right about that."

They sauntered across the street in the direction of the Larson home where Danny was supposed to pick up Doug at six o'clock that evening.

"At least we can keep on practicing over at your house."

Larry nodded. "Yeh. We can play all summer if we want to. But it won't be the same."

There was a long, miserable silence.

"Are you going out for baseball, Larry?" Doug asked after a time.

His friend shook his head. "I don't know for sure. That's something I haven't decided yet. How about you?"

"I don't know either. And to tell you the truth, I don't much care whether I go out or not. I don't think I'd even consider it if the coach hadn't come around this afternoon and talked to me about it."

"He came to see me, too," Larry broke in.

"I guess he's having a rough time getting enough guys out for baseball to make a good team. I told him I wanted to talk to you first; and if you were going out, I thought I'd give it a try, too."

Briefly Larry considered the matter.

"That's funny. I've been waiting to see what you would do. If you go out for baseball, I'll go, too."

Doug's eyes brightened. "Boy, that's swell! I feel better about it already."

They walked down the wide street together. It was almost warm that afternoon. The temperature was above freezing, and little rivulets of water made their way from the drifts to the nearest storm drains. The snow, almost black from the grime of the past few months, was about gone; and the sun shone brightly from a cloudless sky.

Larry spoke once more. "What position are you going out for?"

Doug shrugged. "I haven't played enough baseball to know what I'd like best. To tell you the truth, I've got a hunch I'll be lucky to play well enough to get any position."

When Doug and Danny got home a little later that evening, Del was sitting on the back step, working with Blackie. By this time, the crow was so tame that he didn't have to be kept in a cage. Blackie would wait for Del in a nearby tree and come swooping down to him as soon as he saw him coming up the lane from the school bus.

When Del saw his brother getting out of the car with Danny, he spoke to the crow, "Hello, Blackie, hello."

The crow cocked his head to one side. "Hello. Hello."

Del glanced at Doug and grinned. *That should wake him up a little.*

"Hi. What do you think of that?"

His brother did not answer him.

"Now, let's try something else, Blackie. Blackie is a good crow. Blackie is a good crow."

Doug snickered. "You don't really think you're going to get the dumb crow to say a whole sentence, do you? You might get him to speak a couple of words or so, but a whole sentence? I think you must be more stupid than Blackie."

Del's cheeks flushed hotly. "Danny taught his crow to say a lot of things."

"But you're not Danny." There was a sneer in his voice.

"Maybe not," Del retorted, "but Barney and I

taught Blackie to say 'hello' when you insisted that we'd never be able to get him to say a word. And we're going to keep working on him. What's more, we're going to teach him to say all the things Danny's crow said. You just wait."

Doug sat down on the top step, a superior little smile twisting the corners of his mouth. "Well, when you get him to say more than 'hello,' bring him around. I'd like to hear him."

"You just wait," Del promised defensively. "You will get a chance to hear him. I'll promise you that right now. Give us a little more time and he'll give you a demonstration you won't be forgetting."

Doug snorted. "I don't know why you mess around with that dumb crow when you could be out for sports and having some real fun."

Del bristled suddenly. "It's just that I happen to enjoy working with Blackie! Is that all right?"

For the space of a minute or two the Davis brothers stared hotly at each other, anger flecking their cheeks.

At last Del spoke. "I don't say anything because you want to play basketball every night after school and almost every Saturday. And to tell you the truth, I think it's stupid and a waste of time. So I don't know why you have to get so shook up because I've got Blackie and am teaching him to talk."

Doug shrugged with exaggerated indifference. "Go ahead and play with your stupid crow if you want to. It doesn't make any difference to me. I couldn't care less."

Del would have spoken, but he stopped, lips quivering.

"OK. OK. That's just what I'm going to do. And for your information, I don't care what you think about it. It doesn't make any difference to me!"

A sneer edged Doug's voice. "Oh, no. It doesn't make any difference to you what anybody thinks. You don't have any school spirit or anything!"

"Lay off, will you!" Del's face was pale and his lips were lined with white.

The silence was deafening.

For a moment or two it looked as though Doug was going to continue the argument, but the anger began to leave his face. "Del, why don't you go out for baseball this spring?" he asked bluntly.

"Me go out for baseball?" Incredulity tinged his voice. "That's a laugh!"

"You'd enjoy it."

"Nothing doing. I'm not interested."

"Listen to me for a minute before you start telling me you aren't interested, will you?" Desperation colored his features. "The coach is having a terrible time getting guys to come out for the team. You'd have a swell chance of making the lineup this year. And if you do make the team now, you'd be a cinch to be on it the rest of the time."

Del jerked erect. "So that's it!" He spat out the

words. "Hardly anybody is going out for baseball this year, so you think maybe I might have half a chance of getting to play a little. Big deal!"

"That isn't what I meant." Doug found himself losing his temper again and fought to hold it in check. "It just seems to me that you'd want to take part in *something* that goes on out at school once in a while."

"You can be the hero. I've got other things to do."

Doug ignored the remark.

"Larry and I are going out for baseball," he continued earnestly. "We don't particularly like the game. We'd a lot rather play basketball or football, but we decided to go out anyway. The coach came around and talked to us, and we felt that we should go out and help what we can." He grasped Del by the arm. "You've got just as good a chance to make the team as either of us have. The only thing you've got to do is to try!"

Del's temper fled as quickly as it came. "I'm sorry I spouted off the way I did. But to tell you the truth, Doug, I don't care about baseball. I don't care about playing any game. I've got too many other things that I'd rather do."

With that Doug exploded.

"Yeah!" His lips curled. "You've got too many other things to do! The only reason you don't want to go out for baseball is because I happen to want you to. And you've already decided that you're not going to do anything that makes you associate with me!"

He was so angry his body shook. "Well, if that's the way you feel about it, it doesn't make any difference to me! If you don't want to be with me or the other guys, just don't go out for any sports. Do what you want to do! Fool around with those stupid animals and birds of yours! See if I care!" He turned and stormed away.

Doug didn't know what was the matter with his brother. Del acted as though he didn't even want to be around him or anyone else that Doug especially liked. Del had had a lot of trouble playing basketball, that was true, but Doug had seen him with a baseball. Del had a strong throwing arm and a sharp eye when it came to batting. He could make the baseball team without any trouble if he wanted to.

That was the trouble with Del. He didn't want to make the team. He didn't care if he earned a letter or not.

Doug strode into the house and to the bedroom he and his brother shared. He was glad he hadn't seen Kay or DeeDee. He didn't feel like seeing anyone.

He slammed the door and sat down at their desk. For a long while he stared angrily out the window. He knew that his face was flushed and his breath was coming in short, quick stabs.

After a time Doug began to realize that he shouldn't have gotten mad at Del and talked to him the way he had. Of course, Del shouldn't have gotten mad at him, either. But it had been mostly his own fault.

He had started the trouble by making fun of Blackie and the way Del was working with him. Actually, he hadn't felt the way he sounded about the crow at all. He was proud of the way Del had tamed Blackie and was beginning to get him to talk. He was a little jealous of him, too. No one else they knew had a pet talking crow. When he stopped to think of it, that was really something.

As a Christian, he shouldn't have talked to Del the way he had, Doug realized now. Suddenly he felt sick inside. He got to his feet quickly and went into the living room where DeeDee was curled on the divan, reading a book.

"Hi, DeeDee. Have you seen Del?"

Without looking up she shook her head. "He was on the step when I came home."

"He was on the step when I came home, too, but he's not there now."

"Maybe he took Blackie over to Barney's," she said, "or went out to see if Jumper is all right."

Doug went out to the shed where his brother kept his tame crow, but neither Blackie nor Del was there. They weren't in the barn, either. Maybe they had gone to Barney's, after all. Reluctantly he went back to the house. He wished Del was around. Now that he realized he was in the wrong, he was anxious to get to talk to his brother to tell him how sorry he was for what he had said.

It was almost dark, however, when Del finally

returned to the house. Doug heard the outside door open and went into the living room to meet him.

"Hi." Doug tried to sound as warm and friendly as he could.

Del glanced at him and grunted a curt greeting. He would have pushed by his brother, but Doug stopped him.

"I'd like to talk to you."

Del's eyes narrowed. "What about?" Suspicion laced his voice.

"Come on in the bedroom."

Still, Del did not move.

"I don't know whether I'm going to or not. I don't think I've got anything to say to you."

"It'll only take a minute." Doug pleaded to him with his eyes.

Although Del had protested that he wasn't going into the bedroom, he followed Doug quickly, closing the door behind them. Danny, who had heard the exchange, stared quizzically at them; but he did not ask what was going on.

Once they were alone and the door was closed, Doug turned to his brother.

"I want to apologize to you, Del," he said. "I'm sorry for what I said to you out there a little while ago."

Del's lips trembled, but he made no answer. This was something he hadn't expected.

"I lost my temper when you said you wouldn't go

out for baseball," Doug continued, "and I said a lot of things I shouldn't have said."

Del crossed to the desk and leaned against it, momentarily.

"I know how bad you want me to go out for sports," he admitted, "but I wish you'd understand that I just don't care about them. I never have. I'd much rather be working with Blackie or feeding Jumper or talking with Barney about some of the things he used to do. Besides, look at the horses Uncle Clarence sent us! You hardly spend any time with yours. You're always away playing sports at school."

"I know that." Doug knew he shouldn't say any more, but for some reason he felt that he had to.

"If you'd just go out for one sport, you'd find out how much fun it is. That's all I ask. I want you to get in on some of the good times I get in on."

Del's eyes snapped. "I was out for basketball once. Remember?"

"OK. If that's the way you want it, I guess I haven't got anything more to say about it." He realized Del was furious. "But you're sure missing a good chance for a lot of fun. That's all I've got to say."

Del remained in the room for a long time after Doug left. He, too, was sorry for the way he had acted. Why did he have to get so mad when his brother talked to him? What was the matter with him, anyway?

CHAPTER 5

HIDDEN REASONS

DeeDee was with Sandy Cole as much as ever after Sandy's visit. Sandy usually got to school a few minutes before the bus arrived and waited for her just inside the front door. At noon they always walked down to the lunchroom and ate together. And, as often as not, DeeDee went home with Sandy for an hour or so when school was out in the afternoon. On those occasions Mrs. Cole took her out to the Orlis farm in time for dinner, so she wouldn't have to walk.

DeeDee didn't know how Wally Crowder found out when she would be going to Cole's after school, but he usually seemed to know. He would walk home with them, carrying DeeDee's books and talking about the good time they would have if she would only go to his parties with him.

"I don't get it," he said, his exasperation showing.

"You'll walk home with me, but you won't come to my parties. And that's where we have all the fun, isn't it, Sandy?"

Her friend nodded. "They're groovy."

"I wish you'd come to the next one, DeeDee," Wally pleaded. "It's going to be a real blast."

She managed a crooked smile, but the words stabbed deeply into her heart. She didn't really want to go to any more dances. Not even the ones Wally Crowder had. She had gone to one of his parties, but she hadn't realized there would be dancing. She had been so ill at ease, knowing that her being there was not pleasing to the Lord Jesus Christ.

It wouldn't be right for her to compromise, but, if she continued to refuse to go, what would Wally think? He wouldn't understand about wanting to live a consecrated Christian life, so she couldn't explain to him. The church he went to didn't have convictions about anything. And, more important, what would Sandy think? Would she even want to associate with DeeDee anymore if she turned her back on some of Sandy's best friends?

Wally glanced at DeeDee. "How about it? Will you come to the next party at my place?"

"I–," DeeDee hesitated, coloring slightly.

Sandy spoke up, bitterness edging her young voice. "You can't let Danny and Kay Orlis run your life. You've got to make up your own mind about what you want to do. I don't understand how they can be so nice about some things and so mean about others. They wouldn't let you have any fun at all, if they had their way."

"It isn't that. It–." Her voice trailed away.

Both of her companions were staring at her.

"What is it, then?"

"Didn't you enjoy yourself?" Hurt crept into Wally's voice. "Didn't you have fun when you were at my place for the party a few weeks ago?"

"You know I did." DeeDee was close to tears.

"Then why don't you come to another one?"

DeeDee's lips quivered. She knew what she wanted to tell them. She wanted to say that she didn't want to go to the party because she didn't approve of the things that the kids would be doing, that she felt a Christian young person shouldn't be fooling around with the things of the world. But she didn't dare to do that. If she did, she might lose the friendship of both Sandy and Wally; and she'd just *die* if that happened.

At last Sandy came to her rescue.

"I know how it is for DeeDee at home," she said. "I've been around her house enough to know what Danny and Kay make her do. They're not her real parents, and I guess they don't want her to have any friends or any fun, either. Don't blame DeeDee for not coming to your party. She doesn't dare."

DeeDee's temper flickered. She had thought the same thing about Danny and Kay, but this was different. She couldn't let Sandy or anyone else talk about them that way.

"It isn't as bad as all that," she countered.

"It is, too. You're just too kind and sweet to say how it is for you at home. I've been around Danny and Kay enough to know how they want to know everything you do. And I know what they'd say to you if you went to Wally's party and they found out that you'd been dancing."

Wally shook his head in disbelief. He had never come across anyone quite like that. But he seemed satisfied with the explanation and didn't seem to notice that DeeDee was disturbed by what her friend had said.

"We'll just have to figure out some way of getting you to my parties, anyway," he went on. "We can't have them treating you like a two-year-old and get away with it."

DeeDee would have protested again, but Sandy broke in quickly, changing the subject.

DeeDee's shame grew as she went home that night. It was true that she had told them she wouldn't be able to go to Wally's next party, but she hadn't given them any explanation. She had hedged instead of telling them the reason wasn't because of Danny and Kay's disapproval, but that she had decided she wanted to live the way God directed. She had even let them think she was afraid to go because of Danny and Kay, and that wasn't it, at all. The lump in DeeDee's throat continued to grow. Why did she continually do things like that? She really wanted to have a good Christian testimony. Why was she so weak?

* * *

Although DeeDee had problems of her own, she knew there was something that had been bothering Sandy Cole for some time. Sandy still tried to laugh and joke the way she always had; but the joy had gone out of her eyes, and she wasn't as happy as she had been a few months before. DeeDee wanted to say something to her about it. She had even thought about mentioning it to Danny and Kay and getting them to talk to her friend, but she didn't dare. Sandy didn't understand Danny and Kay at all. She would only think they were trying to interfere with her life.

Finally, however, DeeDee became so burdened for her friend that she tried to find out directly what was troubling Sandy.

Her friend stared incredulously at her in response to her question. " 'What's the matter?' " Her voice echoed DeeDee's words. "I don't know what you mean."

DeeDee hadn't expected a response like that and was startled. "I–I don't know for sure."

She wished that she hadn't said anything about it at all; but now that she began, she had to continue. "Maybe it's my imagination, but it seems to me that you've been acting so–so sad the last week or two. I've been afraid that something's wrong."

Sandy forced a thin laugh. "Oh, no. There's nothing wrong. Nothing at all. I've been studying a little harder than usual, maybe, and–and–." She swallowed hard.

DeeDee could see that it was an effort for her to continue.

"But there's nothing wrong, that's for sure. I've been happier than I've ever been. To tell you the truth, I've been having a blast since you've started going with Wally."

DeeDee eyed her narrowly. What her friend said didn't seem true, somehow. The hurt in her eyes was even deeper than before; and she protested so desperately that everything was all right, it made DeeDee doubt her. In spite of Sandy's protestations, DeeDee was even more concerned about her friend after she talked with her. And the worst of it was that Sandy obviously wasn't going to say anything to DeeDee, or anyone else, about it, so she wouldn't have an opportunity to help her. Sandy was determined to keep her troubles to herself.

* * *

The school in Fairview was buzzing excitedly about the all-school party that was to be held the following Thursday night. As soon as the date was announced, Sandy sought out DeeDee and asked if she was going.

DeeDee hesitated. "I–I don't know for sure."

Sandy bristled. "You don't mean to tell me that Danny and Kay Orlis won't even let you go to a school party, do you?"

"It isn't anything like that," she replied defensively. She was thinking what she had been taught at home and in church about demonstrating her love for God. "It–it just depends–."

Sandy shook her head incredulously, as though she was beginning to see a new dimension to DeeDee's character that she had never seen before.

"I wish I could make you out. Right now, you're acting as though you don't even enjoy going to parties."

DeeDee did not answer her.

"I can tell you this much," Sandy went on. "Wally Crowder's going to be terribly disappointed if you're not there. I talked with him about the party yesterday when it was announced. The first thing he asked me was about you. He wanted to know if you were going to be going."

DeeDee rubbed at her throat uneasily. She had been expecting that; but when it came, she found that she wasn't prepared for it. Before she could speak, Sandy continued.

"Well, you're not going to have to worry about getting into trouble with your jailers over this party. It's not going to be a dance."

DeeDee brightened noticeably. That would make everything different, she reasoned. She wouldn't have to concern herself about what she would do if Wally Crowder should ask her to dance. But she couldn't say anything to Sandy about that, or she would think she was odd.

"I–I'll have to see about the party, Sandy," she said. "I'll let you know in a few days."

"Well, you'd better not wait too long before you make up your mind," her friend told her. "Wally just might get the idea you don't want to go with him and get himself another date."

When DeeDee got home that night, she talked with Danny about getting a new party dress. That was something she would have to have if she was going to be able to go with Wally. She didn't have anything nice enough to wear on a date with him. She thought first about talking with Kay about it but finally decided that Danny might be easier to persuade. She went to him in the living room while they were waiting for Kay to call them to supper and told him about the party.

"And I don't have a thing to wear to the party Thursday night." She smiled winsomely. "I just have to have a new dress for it, Danny."

He laid aside the paper.

"What's the matter with the dress you wore to church last Sunday? I thought it looked real nice."

"That thing?" She wrinkled her nose. "I couldn't wear it, Danny. It's just a rag."

"It looked like a pretty 'rag' to me."

"You know what I mean."

"Kay and I were talking about your clothes last night, DeeDee," he went on. "She said that you have plenty to last until next school year."

"She was talking about school dresses, and I do have plenty of clothes to wear to school and to church. I only need a new party dress – something I won't be ashamed of."

When Danny replied his voice was quiet and conciliatory, but it was plain that he was not to be moved.

"We talked about your good dresses, too, DeeDee. In fact, Kay showed me a couple of very nice dresses that didn't look as though they had been worn more than two or three times. So, I guess you'll have to struggle along to this party in one of those."

She tried to argue with him, but he wouldn't listen. It didn't do any good for her to try to coax him, either. He refused to change his mind. At last she realized it was hopeless to continue and got to her feet angrily.

"Then I'll just stay home from the party!" she announced.

"You can suit yourself about that." He picked up the paper and opened it to the sports page.

DeeDee stormed into her room and closed the door. Angry thoughts clouded her mind. If she still lived with Aunt Carmen, she'd have a new dress. That was one thing for sure. She'd probably have a whole closet full of new dresses. She didn't know why Danny and Kay had to horn in and get her and the boys to live with them. They didn't care whether she had a good time at school parties or not. It didn't matter to them if she never had a good time.

DeeDee stomped over to the bed and sat down on the side of it. If this was something that was going on at church, she told herself, it would be different. They'd get her anything she wanted, if it was for young peoples' or Sunday school.

Well, she'd fix them this time! She wouldn't go to the stupid party. That was all there was to it! She'd stay at home before she'd go in those rags she had!

CHAPTER 6

TEARS OVERFLOW

Ever since Robin got the letter from her mother, she had been praying about getting Alex to go to church with her. Still, she hesitated to say anything to him about it. If only he wasn't so bitter in his opposition to the church and the things of God!

Early in the week she started to hint at her own desire to attend church once more. She knew he loved her a great deal and wanted her to be happy. Perhaps this would have an effect on him.

"Not going to church on Sunday really bothers me, Alex," she said, eyeing him speculatively. "It ruins my whole day."

He looked up from the paper but did not comment.

"I really would like to start going again."

He snorted disdainfully. "Not me. When Sunday comes, I'm bushed. I'm ready to sack in until noon."

She hesitated thoughtfully. "You could sleep Sunday afternoon, Alex," she reminded him.

"I suppose I could, but I'm not going to."

She laid a hand on his arm. "Please, Alex?"

"Now don't start that again." Disgust edged his voice. "I've already told you a hundred times that going to church with you is one place where I'm going to draw the line. So, just lay off, will you? I get tired of all this nagging."

She turned to hide the tears in her eyes. Why did he have to be that way? Why couldn't he go to church with her the way other men go with their wives?

* * *

DeeDee remained in her room, pouting, until Kay called her for supper. Even then, she didn't come out until she had been called two or three times. When she finally came to the kitchen, her mouth was set into a hard line and her eyes were blazing.

Del read the anger in her face. "Who've you been fighting with?"

She did not reply.

"Where's the war, DeeDee?" he persisted. "Who's going to get killed?"

Her stare was withering. "Don't be so infantile!"

Danny suddenly became aware of the conversation. "Del," he said sternly, "knock it off."

DeeDee wrinkled her nose at her brother, but

neither Danny nor Kay saw her. Conversation was strained at the table during the rest of the meal; and as soon as Danny finished with their evening Bible reading and prayer, DeeDee cleared the dishes from the table and began to wash them.

"If you'll wait a moment," Kay said, "I'll help you."

"I'll do them." A lone tear streaked down her reddened cheek. "I have to do everything around here!"

One of her brothers snickered, but she didn't look around. She wasn't going to give them the satisfaction of seeing how she felt. They wouldn't understand, anyway. They thought she was stupid for going to parties and having a good time. As soon as the dishes were done, she went to her room and threw herself on the bed, sobbing silently into her pillow.

The next morning she was quiet and restrained when she got up, speaking only when she was spoken to. She professed not to be hungry and ate only a small piece of toast for breakfast.

At school that morning Sandy knew there was something wrong the instant she saw her.

"What's the matter, DeeDee?" she asked, keeping her voice low.

DeeDee looked at her. She could not speak immediately. Hot, scalding tears came up into her eyes.

"Sometimes I get so mad at that Danny Orlis I could scream!"

In Sandy she found a sympathetic listener. The blonde girl nodded her understanding.

"What is it this time?" she asked. "Doesn't he want you to go to the party?"

DeeDee shook her head. "That isn't it."

"Then what is it?"

DeeDee swallowed at the lump that refused to leave her throat. "He says I've got so many clothes it isn't necessary for me to have a new dress for the party."

Sandy shook her head incredulously, as though she couldn't understand anyone being so cruel. The two girls went into the cafeteria and sat down together, choosing a table in the corner where there was enough privacy so they could talk.

"Danny sounds the way my daddy used to," Sandy began. "He used to be that way to me. He never wanted me to have anything."

DeeDee stared at her. "But I thought–" In her mind she could see Sandy's closet so filled with dresses that there was scarcely room for anything more.

"Mom took care of that," Sandy went on. "She took me into the cities and got me the dresses I had to have, anyway. She charged them and he paid the bills." Sandy laughed. "He didn't even know the difference."

DeeDee thought about that. It wouldn't work with Danny because Kay Orlis wouldn't do that sort of thing. Kay and Danny talked over everything they did, and neither of them ever countermanded what the kids had been told they could or couldn't do.

"There isn't any way I can get a new dress," DeeDee

continued, "and I'm not going to the party without one. That's all there is to it."

Her friend spoke just above a whisper. "You can't do that, DeeDee. You've got to go to the party. Wally's counting on your being there, and so am I. Neither one of us will have any fun if you're not around."

DeeDee's self-pity was all but overwhelming. "I don't like it any better than you do, but there's no use in talking. I'm not going any place in the old rags that I've got. If Danny wants to ruin everything for me, I'll let him do it. He doesn't want me to enjoy myself, so I'll just stay at home and sit. Then maybe he'll be satisfied."

Sandy thought for a moment. "I don't know why we didn't think of it before!" she exclaimed.

DeeDee looked at her friend in surprise.

"You won't have to stay home from the party, and you won't have to worry about a new dress, either. You can wear something of mine! I've got a whole closet full of them!"

DeeDee stared at her, eyes widening. "You–you mean that I can wear one of your dresses again – like I did for Wally's party?"

"I don't know why not. I've got a whole raft of them hanging in the closet. I've got a lot of dresses that I've only worn once or twice, so nobody will recognize them. They're just like new!"

"But–."

"It's all settled." Sandy straightened. "And it isn't

going to do you any good to argue with me. I'm telling you right now that you're going to wear one of my dresses."

DeeDee's eyes filled with tears. "Sandy, you're the best friend I've ever had!"

"And you're the best friend I've ever had, so it's all settled. We'll show that Danny Orlis that he's not going to keep you from the party!"

DeeDee's hurt fled. It wouldn't make any difference that she would be wearing a dress that belonged to Sandy. It was like Sandy said: she had so many dresses no one could remember them all. And Sandy was too close a friend to tell anyone that DeeDee was wearing one of her dresses. Everything was perfect.

A smile teased the corners of her mouth. She wondered, idly, what Danny would think when he saw that she had a new dress to wear, even if he was so close with his money and so lacking in understanding that he refused to buy her one. She'd show him that he couldn't run her life! She had ways of getting what she wanted in spite of him.

The day of the party finally arrived. DeeDee and Sandy planned that she would stay at the Cole house for dinner and go to the party from there. However, when she mentioned it to Kay that morning before going to school, Kay surprised her by refusing.

"I don't believe you had better stay with Sandy tonight, DeeDee," she said.

Panic gripped her. "But I'm not going to stay all

night. I just wanted to accept Sandy's invitation to have dinner with them. Then I could go to the party from there."

"I understand that," Kay replied, "but I still think you had better come home."

The girl pouted. "But why?"

"I feel that it's best, DeeDee," she answered. "That's all."

"I'll just have to turn around and go right back to Fairview after supper. I could just as well stay with Sandy and go to the party from there. It would save Danny a trip."

"He'll have to take the boys in to the party anyway. He might just as well take you. too."

DeeDee's lower lip trembled. "I suppose this is part of the way you and Danny trust me," she said, her voice quavering.

Kay did not answer her.

At school DeeDee told Sandy what Kay had said.

"So I won't be able to wear your dress, after all."

Sandy thought for a moment. "Oh, yes you can. You can go over to the house after school and pick it up. You don't have to stay at my house in order to wear one of my dresses."

But DeeDee still didn't see how it could work out. "I thought you were going to get your hair fixed after school. You won't be able to go home with me to get one for me."

A pout pulled at the corners of Sandy's mouth, but only for an instant.

"I'd forgotten all about that, but that won't make any difference. You can go out to the house after school anyway. If Mom isn't home, you can go in and get one of my dresses. You've been in my room often enough to know where they are."

"Are you sure it'll be all right?" DeeDee asked uncertainly.

"Of course it will. You can take any of the dresses except for the one that's still in the plastic bag from the store. Mother and I went down and got me a new dress the day before yesterday."

DeeDee sighed her relief. "I don't know what I'd ever do without you."

Sandy's smile faded, replaced by a new serious set to her mouth. "I don't know what I'd do without you, either."

That afternoon when school was out, the girls met once more at their lockers.

"I just remembered something," Sandy said. "I remember for sure that Mother isn't going to be home this afternoon. You'll have to have my house key."

DeeDee took it reluctantly. She felt strange taking the key to Sandy's house so she could go in and borrow a dress. "Are you sure it will be all right with your parents?"

"Of course it'll be all right with them. They aren't

like Danny and Kay. They let me do anything I want to."

DeeDee went over to the Cole home as quickly as possible. She would have to hurry if she was going to get the dress and still walk out to the farm for dinner.

On the way she thought about Sandy. There wasn't another girl in the whole school who would do for her what Sandy had done that day. Of course, Danny and Kay didn't like Sandy, DeeDee decided. She could tell that by the way they acted. But that didn't make any difference. She couldn't have a better friend than Sandy, and she was going to keep on running around with her. She didn't care what they said.

On the steps of the big house DeeDee paused momentarily. At first, she was about to ring the doorbell, but there was no car in the driveway and the garage door was closed. As Sandy said, her mother must have gone out.

DeeDee opened the front door and went inside. She didn't like doing that, even though Sandy had given her the key and insisted that she use it. If she hadn't wanted the dress so badly, she would have gone back to the farm without it. But Sandy had insisted that it was all right for her to go into the house and pick out a dress she liked, so there could be nothing wrong with it.

DeeDee was about to go up the steps when she heard a faint sound from the opposite side of the living room. She stopped, turning quickly. There was a slight figure lying on the divan. At first she didn't recognize who it was. She stiffened, her heart pounding fiercely. Then she saw that it was Sandy's mother.

"Mrs. Cole!"

There was no answer.

"Mrs. Cole! What's the matter? What's wrong?"

By this time DeeDee saw that the woman's shoulders were twitching convulsively. She ran over to her.

"Mrs. Cole! Are you alright?"

Slowly the older woman became aware of the fact that DeeDee was in the room. She managed to stop crying and straightened slowly, wiping at her eyes with a small, knotted handkerchief.

"DeeDee!" she exclaimed. "What are you doing here?"

DeeDee swallowed against the lump in her throat. "Sandy told me that I could borrow one of her dresses to wear to the party tonight." The words tumbled out defensively, as though Sandy's mother might think she had sneaked into the house for some other purpose. "She was going to come with me, but she had an appointment to get her hair fixed. So she–she gave me the key to come in and pick out one." Her voice weakened. "She–she said it would be all right."

"Of course it is." Mrs. Cole continued to dab at her eyes. She seemed to be more concerned about something else. "I–I'm awfully sorry that you saw me like this. I–."

The girl looked deeply into her eyes. "Is there anything I can do?"

Sandy's mother managed a weak smile.

"I–I suppose I do owe you some sort of an explanation." She fumbled for words. "I've had such a miserable headache, I couldn't help crying."

DeeDee nodded sympathetically. "My mother used to get bad headaches sometimes when we lived in Guatemala."

"I–I don't know when I've had such a headache that it made me cry this way," Mrs. Cole said lamely.

DeeDee took a deep breath. "Is there anything I can do for you?"

Sandy's mother shook her head.

"No, there's nothing anyone can do." There was quiet desperation in her voice. "But I–I think I feel a little better now." She got shakily to her feet and crossed to the other side of the room where she straightened a picture on the wall. "Now, what was it you wanted? One of Sandy's dresses?"

The girl paused. "I don't have to have it. I can wear one of my own."

Mrs. Cole's smile came on, warm and friendly.

"Of course you can have one of Sandy's dresses to wear to the party tonight." She came over and put her arm about DeeDee's shoulder. "Let's go up and see if we can find one that will be just right for you."

The Davis girl glanced at her obliquely. She could see by the way Mrs. Cole was acting that she desperately wanted DeeDee to believe that she had been crying because her head ached so badly.

However, DeeDee knew better. She could tell by the hurt in the woman's eyes that there was some other reason for the convulsive sobbing.

DeeDee drew in a deep breath. This might have something to do with the sadness she had been seeing in Sandy's eyes the last few weeks. Her own uneasiness for her best friend continued to grow.

CHAPTER 7

LOVING OPPOSITION

DeeDee picked out a dress from Sandy's closet, tried it on hurriedly to be sure that it fit, and left the Cole home as quickly as possible. Sandy's mother followed her to the door.

"Thank you, Mrs. Cole," she said. "Thank you so very much. You'll never know how much this means to me."

"That's all right." Her smile was fleeting. "That's little enough to do for you."

"That isn't the way I feel about it. I–I couldn't have gone to the party tonight without this dress. I don't have a thing that's nice enough to wear."

Mrs. Cole clucked understandingly. "I'm just glad that Sandy has been able to help you." She waited until the girl was out on the sidewalk. Then she suddenly stepped out to the edge of the porch and called out quickly. "DeeDee."

"Yes?" She turned and looked back.

For an instant or two the woman was silent, curiosity gleaming in her eyes. Then she seemed to change her mind. Her smile came back again.

"Oh, nothing. Go on to the party and enjoy yourself."

DeeDee shifted the dress box from one arm to the other and quickened her pace. It was a long walk out to the farm, and she had stayed so long at the Coles' that the time was getting late. She would have to hurry or she would be late for dinner, and Danny would scold her about that.

As she walked, however, her thoughts were not on Danny or the party and the dress she was going to wear. She couldn't help thinking about the Cole house. There was something terribly wrong there. DeeDee was convinced of that, in spite of Sandy's efforts to keep it from her. DeeDee had never had bad headaches herself, but she remembered those her mother used to have. She used to get so sick with them that she was in bed for two or three days, but DeeDee could never remember hearing her cry with one.

No, she was convinced that the tears had to be caused by something else. Something that must be very serious to cause her to be so upset.

Then DeeDee thought about Danny and Kay. Maybe they could help Mrs. Cole with her problems. They had been able to help a lot of people. But, as soon as the thought came, she decided it would never do to have either of them try and talk with her. Danny and Kay would never be able to influence a person as wealthy, poised, and confident as Mrs. Cole.

When she got home, Danny was in the living room reading the evening paper. He looked up as she came in.

"Hello, DeeDee."

She spoke to him, a thin edge to her voice to remind him that she hadn't forgotten how unreasonable he had been over getting her a new dress for the school party.

He noticed the box.

"What've you got there?" There was no anger in his voice. Only curiosity.

Color stained her cheeks.

"Nothing that would interest you," she retorted testily.

"Why don't you try me and see if I'm interested?"

"If you must know, it's a dress to wear to the party tonight."

Danny Orlis frowned. "I thought we went over that and decided that you weren't to buy a new dress now, DeeDee."

She bristled peevishly. She might have known he would act this way.

"For your information I didn't buy a new dress. Sandy Cole and her mother let me borrow one of hers." With that she stalked into her bedroom and closed the door.

When she came out some ten or fifteen minutes later, Danny put down his paper.

"DeeDee."

She glanced in his direction, temper glinting in her eyes. "Yes?"

"I'd like to talk to you for a minute."

She stomped to a chair and dropped into it. "I have to hurry. The party starts at 7:30."

"We'll be there in plenty of time," he told her. "Right now, I'd like to talk to you about that dress you just brought home."

"What about it?" Her defenses were up.

"I thought we had decided that you have some dresses in your closet that are nice enough to wear to the party tonight."

"You're the one who said they were all right to wear." Anger scalded her words. "As for me, I wouldn't be caught dead in one of them." Her smile was both defiant and triumphant. "And now I don't have to. I'm going to wear one of Sandy's dresses."

Danny's expression did not change and his voice remained as calm as ever, but she knew from the tone he used that it would do no good for her to try to argue with him. "I don't want you to wear Sandy's dress, DeeDee," he said.

Her eyes widened. "Danny!"

"I'm sorry about this because I know that you'd

like to wear it, but we're financially able to get you the clothes you need, DeeDee. It isn't necessary for you to borrow dresses from someone else."

She stared incredulously at him as though she had never heard anything so unreasonable.

"I don't see why it should matter to you, Danny," she told him. "Mrs. Cole doesn't care. She went up to Sandy's room with me and helped me pick out the dress that looked best on me. She said I could come up and borrow dresses from Sandy anytime I wanted to. She's got a whole closetful that she hardly ever wears."

Danny smiled to soften his words. "Maybe she doesn't care, DeeDee, but in this particular case I care very much. Kay and I decided that the dresses you have are nice enough for the party. And we don't want you to borrow from Sandy Cole. Is that clear?"

The girl's anger flared.

"You just don't want me to go to the party and have any fun!" she retorted accusingly. "You're saying that so you can have your own way."

"That isn't it, at all." Danny's voice was still calm. "But I can tell you, DeeDee, this sort of arguing is getting you nowhere. Kay and I have made up our minds regarding this and all the talking you try to do isn't going to change us. So, I think it would be just as well that you stop now before you say something that will cause me to punish you."

She straightened indignantly. "I've never heard

of such a thing!" Tears flooded her eyes. "If I can't wear Sandy's dress, I won't go! That's all there is to it!" With that she whirled and dashed from the room.

After a few minutes Kay came into the living room where Danny was sitting alone. He had gone back to the evening paper.

"I thought I heard DeeDee in here with you a few minutes ago."

"You did." He folded his paper and laid it aside.

"When she didn't come home on the bus, I was afraid she would be late for dinner. I'm glad she's home. We're ready to eat."

"DeeDee and I had a little disagreement about a party dress I said she couldn't wear." Danny told her what had taken place.

Kay sat down momentarily. "I hadn't heard any more about a party dress for tonight, and I thought she had forgotten about it."

"Not DeeDee. She's going to get her own way through one scheme or another. I really was sorry that I wasn't able to let her wear Sandy's dress to the party. In a way, it probably wouldn't have hurt anything, except that we had told her she has dresses that are plenty nice enough for a school party."

Kay Orlis took a deep breath. "It isn't good for her to be able to borrow clothes from someone like Sandy. The Cole family has so much money and Sandy is able to get so much of everything that DeeDee is already finding fault with the things we have and what we're able to do for her."

Danny nodded. "Before you came in, I was sitting here trying to figure out if I was just being mean or if I was justified in insisting that DeeDee wear her own clothes. The way I look at it, though, is that there are some kids who can borrow clothes once in a while, and it doesn't seem to hurt them at all, but DeeDee is different."

"I suppose most girls go through a period when they borrow clothes from a girlfriend or an older or younger sister," Kay said. "I know I did. But it does seem to have an effect on DeeDee that isn't good."

"That's just the way I feel about it. She's too easily swayed by expensive things. If we let her go on borrowing Sandy's clothes, I can see her being hurt a great deal. She could easily get to the place where she would feel that she had to have much more of everything than we are able to get her."

Kay got to her feet. "I'm glad you stayed firm, Danny. I know it's best for DeeDee this way."

She went to the bedroom door and knocked. "DeeDee, it's time for dinner."

There was no answer.

"DeeDee!" Her voice raised.

"I'm not hungry," DeeDee muttered, just loud enough to be heard.

Kay started to say more, but Danny motioned to her that he thought it best to allow DeeDee to remain in her room until she was ready to come out. They went into the kitchen where the boys were already sitting at the table.

Del's gaze fastened curiously on Danny. "Where's DeeDee? Isn't she going to eat with us tonight?"

"I don't think so. At least, she won't be eating with us for a while."

Her brother snorted. "What's eating her now? Does she want to date that Wally Crowder again and you won't let her?"

Danny pulled out a chair and sat down at the table.

"Let's say this is a personal matter between DeeDee and Kay and me. OK?"

"I just asked."

Danny did not reply.

After the blessing he turned to Doug and asked about the baseball team Fairview was going to have that spring.

"OK, I guess," Doug replied. "We've got a real good pitcher and catcher, and the first baseman isn't too bad. We should do all right."

Del broke in irritably. "I suppose you're pitching or catching, so that's the reason those positions are going to be all right." He tried to sound as though he was joking, but there was a barb in his voice.

Danny and Doug pretended not to notice Del's biting tone.

"Nope," Doug answered, "I'm playing left field. Or I should say that I'm trying to play left field. I don't even know whether I'll be good enough to hold down that position. I haven't done too well yet."

For a time nobody spoke. Del was surprised to hear Doug talk that way. Maybe Doug wasn't so good at baseball after all. For an instant he almost wished that he had tried out for the team. It would have been good to beat Doug out, just once.

Then Kay turned her attention to him. "How are you and Blackie making out these days? I haven't heard you say anything about him for a week or two. Is he learning any more new words?"

Del shook his head. "Sometimes I think he talks the way Doug says he plays baseball. He acts as though he's out in left field somewhere."

Everyone laughed.

"Just don't get discouraged. If you keep working with him, he'll learn," Danny said. "It just takes time."

"You're going to have to bring him in again and have him give us a demonstration."

Del shook his head emphatically. "Not until he talks a lot better than he does now. If I got him in here, the chances are that he wouldn't say a word and I'd feel like a fool."

CHAPTER 8

DEEDEE'S SELF-CONSOLATION

DeeDee didn't come out of her room anymore that night, and the next morning when she got up for breakfast she was cold and reserved. But self-consoling thoughts boiled within her.

Danny and Kay were all right in their own way, she told herself petulantly. They tried to make her and the boys happy, and they did take care of them. But it wasn't like having a real mother and dad. If her parents were still alive, she wouldn't have the terrible problems she had now. Her real parents had really loved her and Doug and Del, and would have been concerned that they have good times. They wouldn't have made her stay home from a party so they could have their own way. That was sure!

Danny and Kay only pretended to love her, she was sure now. Something like this showed how they really felt. Well, if that was the way they wanted it, she guessed that was the way it would have to be. There wasn't anything she could do about it.

She could scarcely bear to think about going to school that morning and letting Sandy and Wally and the other kids know how shamefully Danny and Kay actually treated her. In a way it made her ashamed for them that they were so stubborn and so narrow-minded.

She could have understood their not being able to afford a new dress for her. That sort of thing used to happen often when her parents were still alive. The thing that made her so furious was that it wouldn't have cost them anything to have let her wear Sandy's dress. In fact, it would have saved them money. Danny was just stubborn and determined to have his own way, that was all she could figure out!

But, if that was the way he wanted to treat her, it was all right with her. She had already had a lot of rough knocks. She could take this one, too, until she got old enough to go out on her own.

DeeDee finished eating and went to her room for her books and sweater. She was just coming back into the living room when Danny opened the door.

"I'm going to the airport this morning, DeeDee," he said. "I can drop you off at school on the way, if you want to go a little early."

She looked up. "No, thank you.".

"I'll have you there fifteen minutes before the bus does."

DeeDee noted his remark with satisfaction. So, he was feeling sorry for what he had done to her and was trying to make it up to her. Well, if he thought he could square things by giving her a ride to school, he was badly mistaken. Maybe this dress incident wasn't the most important thing that had happened since they moved to Fairview to live with Danny and Kay, but it told her a lot of things. Things she hadn't realized before. She knew now what Danny thought of her. And that was something! She wasn't going to let him do anything more for her than she had to.

"I'll wait for the bus, thank you." Her voice was iced.

"Okay." Danny shrugged indifferently. "Suit yourself."

She went out to the road and waited for the school bus, turning her back when Danny drove by with the boys a couple of minutes later. Somehow, she had always thought she was someone special to him. She had felt that he was one person who understood her and wanted to help her. That was what made this so hard!

Danny had probably decided now that he didn't want to have her around anymore. If that was it, she just might quit school and get a job. Then she could pay room and board, and buy her own clothes. She wouldn't have to go to him for anything. That should make him happy!

Only he'd probably get mad then because he

didn't have control over her anymore. He wouldn't like it because he wouldn't be able to make her do everything he wanted her to.

The more DeeDee thought about what had happened, the bigger her case against Danny loomed. When she got to school, she was almost in tears.

Sandy, who had been waiting for her as usual, hurried up to her.

"DeeDee! What happened that you didn't get to the party last night? Wally and I looked all over for you, but you didn't come."

DeeDee's gaze met hers, miserably. She tried to speak, but for the moment she could not.

"I thought you must be sick or something."

"Oh, no, it was nothing like that." She swallowed the lump that persisted in staying in her throat. "If you must know, it–it was Danny."

Sandy's gaze narrowed. "What did he do this time?" Her tone made it apparent that she expected something terrible.

"He wouldn't let me wear the dress you and your mother loaned me!"

Sandy stared as though she couldn't believe it. "But why?"

"He didn't say." Tears trembled on her eyelids.

"He just told me that I couldn't wear it."

"What difference could it possibly make to him whether you wore a dress of mine to the party or one of your own?"

DeeDee shook her head. "To tell you the truth, I don't know why Danny does half the things he does. I think he wants to get back at me for something. He said that I had to wear the clothes he and Kay bought for me or I–I couldn't go to the party. So I didn't go!"

"I don't blame you. I wouldn't have gone, either." They started down the hall towards their homeroom. "I've never heard of such a thing. He should be glad that you could wear one of my dresses and look nice. They cost twice as much as anything he ever bought for you." Her expression changed. "But I suppose that's just one of the things you have to put up with because your parents are–are dead and the court awarded you to Danny and Kay. They wouldn't do that sort of thing to you if you were their own daughter."

"That's what I think, too." DeeDee looked at Sandy gratefully. At least she had one friend who understood her.

They were almost at their homeroom when DeeDee remembered how sick Mrs. Cole had been when she went to get the dress. And, in spite of that, Mrs. Cole had gone up to Sandy's room and helped her find something. DeeDee was ashamed of herself for thinking only of her own troubles.

"I forgot to ask about your mother," she said. "How's her headache?"

Sandy's forehead crinkled. "Her headache?"

"When I stopped to pick up the dress, she said that she had a terrible headache." DeeDee took a deep breath. "She had such a bad headache, that she was lying on the divan in the living room, crying."

"Oh!" Sandy spoke quickly.

A little too quickly, it seemed to DeeDee, as though she had something she wanted to hide.

"Oh, I remember now. I guess I was so excited about the party that I had forgotten all about it." Sandy managed a thin smile. "Her headache was almost gone this morning. In fact, I think it was gone. She didn't say anything about it."

DeeDee couldn't help noticing that the mention of her mother caused Sandy's expression to change. The lights in her eyes died away, and a mysterious sadness took their places. For the moment DeeDee forgot how badly Danny treated her. There was something wrong with Sandy. She didn't know what it was, but it had to be something very important.

* * *

There was no doubt about the fact that Doug was not nearly as good at baseball as he was at basketball. That was unusual, too. He and Del had played catch by the hour when they lived with their parents in Guatemala, while he had never had a basketball in his hands until they moved to Fairview not long before.

Doug's throwing arm was strong enough, but he didn't have the eye for batting and he had trouble judging flies. More often than not he would lose sight of the ball against the sky or figure that it was going to drop a dozen feet short of where it usually came down. However, he did manage to make the team as an outfielder – much to his own surprise.

"I think they ran out of material, Danny," he said at home, "and figured I was the only guy available for the position."

"I wouldn't go so far as to say that," Danny replied. "I was talking with the coach a couple of days ago. He said that he's got hopes of your making a good baseball player. He seems to think that the main thing you need right now is confidence and experience."

"I wish I felt as sure about it as that. Right now, the way I look at it, I'm a first-class duffer."

Del, who had been taking an active part in the conversation up to this point, fell silent. He didn't see why everybody made so much over Doug just because he was good at sports. It made him feel as though it didn't do any good for him to try anything. He wasn't a basketball or baseball star, so nobody would pay any attention to anything he did. He got up from the table abruptly and went out to see if he could find Blackie. At least his crow didn't care whether he was able to play baseball or not.

* * *

For all the trouble the coach had that year in getting enough guys to try out for baseball, the Fairview nine did very well. Larry Larson developed rapidly into an excellent pitcher. He won his first game easily and squeaked by in the second on the strength of a sharp double by the first baseman in extra innings.

There had been little interest in baseball around school during the early part of the season. It was almost like the high school debate team – the only ones interested were those taking part. But as the baseball team won their first four games against tough opposition, the student body suddenly became aware of the fact that the school had a good baseball team. Some of the kids even began to talk about winning the conference, and the crowds at the games began to build.

Larry and Doug were on their way home after practice when a couple of older guys gave them a ride. As soon as they got into the car, their friends began to talk with them about the team.

"You've been doing OK, Larry," one of them said. "I didn't know a little shrimp like you could throw as hard as you do."

Doug spoke up. "Larry's the big reason we're undefeated this season."

Larry grinned self-consciously. "Joe's good, too," he said. "A team's got to have more than one good pitcher if they're going to get anywhere."

"I don't know about that. We haven't needed more than one pitcher so far. The way it looks to me, our junior high team is going to win the conference championship."

"Don't hold your breath until we do," Larry replied. "We've got some rugged opposition to meet before we dare to talk that way."

* * *

Robin Smith was home alone the night Rick and Karen Preston called. She thought it was Alex coming home for some books and was slow in answering the knock on the door.

"I was just finishing the dishes. I–." The words caught in her throat. "Oh, I'm sorry. I thought you were Alex."

"No, we're not Alex, but we would like to come in." Rick's smile was warm and cordial.

"Oh–oh, yes." She stepped back and gestured helplessly. "I'm sorry. Won't you come in?"

The handsome young man and his attractive, well-dressed wife looked to Robin to be about the same age as she and Alex. They entered the little apartment, found chairs, and sat down. The young couple introduced themselves to Robin, and for a moment or two they talked about the school and Alex's plans for the future.

"Alex and I have something in common. I was going to be a coach, too," Rick said.

"What happened?" Robin asked. "Didn't you like it?"

"It wasn't that. I found something more important to devote my life to."

"Oh."

Alex probably wouldn't like Rick, Robin reasoned. Her husband didn't claim that coaching was the most important calling in the world, but she did know that it was by far the most important thing in his life. Everything they did, thought, or planned had to reckon with his determination to prepare himself to be a coach. Already he was thinking about which college or university, or maybe a job with one of the pro teams if he got that good.

After a moment Rick continued, "Yes, I discovered that the most important thing in all the world is to present the claims of Christ to those who don't know Him as Savior."

Robin gasped. "You–you're Christians?"

"Is there something strange about that?" Rick asked.

"Oh, no," Robin answered. "There's nothing strange about it. In fact, it's wonderful! For more than a year I've been praying for Christian friends. You see, we've never met another Christian couple on the campus."

Karen spoke up. "I take it that you and your husband are believers."

Robin winced. "I–I wish that was true. You don't know how much I wish that was true. Alex is a wonderful husband, but he simply doesn't have time for the Lord."

"That's the kind of students Karen and I spend most of our time talking to."

"You mean you're–." Robin's voice choked. "It doesn't seem possible."

Rick's laugh was pleasant. "I don't know what you were going to say, but I suppose you could call us missionaries to the kids here at the U."

Tears came to Robin Smith's eyes. "Oh, that's wonderful! You're an answer to prayer!"

CHAPTER 9

ANOTHER TRAP IS SET

Robin Smith kept Rick and Karen Preston in the apartment until almost midnight asking questions about their work. It was thrilling to hear about college guys and girls coming to Christ.

Robin hadn't intended to tell them anything about Alex or their marriage; but after they had been in the apartment for a time, she felt as though she had known them all her life. Before she was aware of what she was doing, she was confiding her concern for Alex with them.

She told the Prestons about their marriage while they were still in high school, how Alex had to quit, and how glad she was when he finally decided to go back and get his diploma so he could go on to college and prepare himself to teach. She even told them about his antagonism to the gospel, how he refused to go to church with her or to have anything to do with the Christians they knew back home. Usually, Robin tried to keep that information from their friends and acquaintances, but she was thankful to be able to share her burden with these young missionaries who had won her confidence so quickly. Before leaving, they had a time of prayer with her, asking God to intervene in her young husband's life.

As they went to leave, she followed them to the door. "I'm so thankful you came tonight. I really believe that you're an answer to prayer."

"Praise the Lord," Karen said.

"Who knows," Robin continued. "Maybe you will be the means of leading Alex to Christ."

Karen laid a hand on Robin's arm, tenderly. "We'll certainly be praying for him."

"Thank you. I appreciate that so much."

Before they left, Robin invited them back for dinner at some future time.

"But I'd like to wait to set the time and the evening," she said, "until I can be sure that Alex will be home."

"Just let us know a day or so ahead, and we'll certainly try to make it," Karen assured her.

It was a long while after they were gone before Robin was able to go to sleep that night. The more she thought about Rick and Karen Preston coming to visit, the more convinced she was that God had sent them. Of all the thousands of students going to the university, why would the Prestons have chosen to come to their place? It wasn't just a coincidence. There had to be a reason for it.

It would be so wonderful if Alex would only accept the Lord as his Savior and take a stand for Him. Then, indeed, her happiness would be complete.

* * *

For that season, at least, Doug quit trying to get his brother, Del, to go out for sports with him. It didn't do any good and only caused trouble between them. He had talked the whole problem over with Danny, who had suggested that Doug try to spend as much time with Del as possible.

"But he doesn't want to do any of the things that I want to do," Doug protested. "That's the thing that makes it so hard."

"Then you'll have to do the things he wants to do," Danny answered, "or give up on him."

Doug frowned. "I don't see why I'm the one who always has to give in. Why can't he do what I want to do once in a while?"

In spite of his protests, however, he went into the bedroom where Del was studying and asked if he was going down to see Barney the following morning.

Del's eyes narrowed. "I don't know for sure. I suppose I'll be going down there as soon as I get my work done. Why?"

"I thought maybe I'd like to ride along with you."

He paused as he saw the expression on his brother's face. "If that's OK."

"If you want to go along, it's sure OK with me." Del frowned quizzically. "But why the interest in Barney all of a sudden? You haven't cared much about going out to see him before now."

Doug bristled. "If you don't want me to go along, just say so. I can probably find something else to do tomorrow."

"You don't need to get so shook up about it," Del replied. "I told you that you're welcome to come along. It just seemed funny that you'd decide you want to go with me tomorrow, that's all. You're the guy who thinks it's stupid to fool around with a crow. Remember?"

"I'll just stay home if that's the way you feel about it." Doug pivoted and started away. "I don't know why I try to do anything with you, anyway. This is the way I usually get treated when I do."

Doug slammed the bedroom door resoundingly. He didn't know what was wrong with that brother of his. He didn't want to go out for sports or have anything to do with him. Del just didn't want to be around him. That was all there was to it.

Doug sat down on the living room couch and opened his history book to study, but the words swam on the page. He'd never say anything else to Del about going anywhere with him again, that was sure. He wouldn't let him have the satisfaction of turning him down another time.

Doug closed the book thoughtfully, and for a long while he stared out the window. He didn't know what was happening between him and Del, but it wasn't good. After all, they were even more than brothers – they were part of a set of triplets. They should be running around together. They shouldn't be at each other's throats the way they were most of the time.

He stood and moved to the table, where he fingered Danny's Bible. It all began when he made the basketball team and Del didn't. That was when he got more interested in sports and Del began to fool around more with animals and birds. Now it seemed as though they hardly knew each other anymore.

After a time, Del came into the living room.

"I–I didn't mean anything by what I said a little while ago, Doug," he stammered.

"That's all right."

"It was just that you've given me such a bad time about Blackie and going out for baseball and everything. I thought you were going to get on my back about something."

Doug shook his head. "I just wanted to go with you tomorrow, that's all." His voice raised. "But if you don't want me to, that's all right. I guess I'll manage to live without it."

"I'd like to have you go with me," Del said, "and

I know that Barney'd like to have you along, too. He asks about you every once in a while."

The other boy hesitated. "Well, if you're sure that you want me, I guess I'll be able to go."

The next morning the boys got up at the usual time and hurried through their chores as soon as breakfast was over. While Del went for Blackie, Doug saddled both horses and led them out into the yard. Most of the time Blackie was out of his cage now, flying about the farm buildings; but when Del took him down to Barney's, he put him in the cage and carried him. Doug only had to wait for him a minute or two before he came, holding Blackie's cage in one hand.

"I guess we're all set," Doug said.

They mounted and rode out of the yard.

"I've got to stop off and look at Jumper first," Del told his brother. "I haven't seen him for a week or two, and I want to be sure that he's all right."

Doug shrugged his shoulders. "That's all right with me. I don't have much else to do today."

It was good being out alone with Del, Doug thought as they rode along the narrow trail that skirted the lake. It seemed like old times in Guatemala when they did everything together. Doug glanced at his brother. He wished things could be that way now. He didn't like the idea of going off in one direction and Del going off in another. They were brothers. It wasn't right that they were so far apart.

* * *

Robin Smith began to plan for the evening when she would have Rick and Karen Preston over for dinner. She had to choose the night carefully. It would have to be at a time when Alex didn't have to study. That was limiting in itself, because it wasn't often that she could be sure he wouldn't have to go to the library or spend the evening writing a paper. She talked with him about it and finally was able to set a night when he was reasonably sure he wouldn't have to study. She called the Prestons, prayerfully, almost afraid to ask them about coming the next evening, because she was afraid they couldn't.

But, as it turned out, they were free and said they would come.

Robin had to work at the store that day, but she did part of the preparation for the evening meal the night before and got up an hour earlier that morning to finish it. She felt a tinge of excitement she hadn't known since the early days of their marriage. This was not just another dinner with guests. This could be the night that would change the entire direction of their lives.

Just having Christians around for an evening would be worth all the effort. It had been months since she had enjoyed any real fellowship with Christians her own age. But for her that night the fellowship was of minor importance. Rick and Karen were a tremendous couple. And if Alex liked them, and there was no reason why he wouldn't, there would be a chance of striking up a lasting friendship. There would be a chance of influencing Alex for Christ.

True, he hadn't shown any inclination to be interested in anything spiritual up to that point, but with a sharp young couple like the Prestons, anything could happen.

Robin could scarcely imagine what it would be like if Alex took a stand for Christ. Everything would be perfect!

She waited for them with growing anticipation.

Alex came home from school a few minutes before their company was to arrive for the evening. He looked around uneasily. "What's going on tonight?" he wanted to know.

"You remember. Rick and Karen Preston are coming over."

He frowned. "Who are they?"

"I told you about them. They stopped by the apartment to visit a week or so ago. I asked you about inviting them over and you said it was all right."

He dropped wearily into a chair and opened a book.

"OK." His own disapproval was evident. "I guess I can put up with them for an evening. But I've got a pile of collateral reading to do."

Her disappointment grew.

"You said you didn't think you would have to study tonight," she countered. "That's why I asked them over this evening. You said you didn't have much studying on Tuesdays."

Disgust edged his voice.

"I said I didn't have *as much* studying on Tuesday.

You've been around the U enough to know that a guy can never tell when he's going to have a pile of work to do. We're going to have a test in the morning, and I've got this collateral reading to do to prepare for it."

Robin was close to tears. "I'm sorry, Alex. Honestly, I am."

He went over and put his arm about her shoulders.

"Now, Robin, don't let it get you down. I know how you feel. And I know it's been hard for you living the way we've had to live and not having money enough to do anything we'd like to. If it'll make you feel better, I'll wait and study after they've gone."

Her smile banished the gloom in her pretty young face. Alex was different than he had been when they were first married. He was softer and more considerate. Surely it would be easier for them to talk with him about the Savior now than it had been at first. She kissed him impulsively.

"Thanks, honey. It isn't hard at all when you understand."

"I understand, all right. And I'm going to make it up to you just as soon as I graduate. You can count on that. You'll never be sorry for the sacrifices you've had to make to help me get through school."

Robin went back to the kitchen, a prayer in her heart. This was probably the most important evening in Alex's whole life. There never had been a time when more had been at stake. Suddenly she could scarcely wait for Rick and Karen to get there, so they could talk to him.

CHAPTER 10

BACKFIRE

Rick and Karen Preston came to the Smith apartment shortly after six o'clock that evening.

"Would you answer the door, Alex?" Robin called from the kitchen.

"I'm on my way."

He introduced himself to their guests and invited them in.

"We're so glad to meet you." Rick's smile was infectious. "Robin has told us so much about you that we've been anxious to get acquainted with you."

The corners of Alex's mouth lifted slightly. "You shouldn't believe everything she says. She's my press agent."

Rick took a chair in the living room, but his wife remained standing.

"I'll go out and see if I can help Robin in the kitchen."

Once she was gone, Alex and Rick talked about the university's prospects for a winning football team the following September. They talked about the classes Alex was taking and the opportunities for a young man in the field of coaching. Alex was surprised at his guest's knowledge of the profession.

"You certainly know a lot about coaching," he said. "Are you going to be a coach, too?"

Rick shook his head. "There was a time when that was all I could think of. I even came to school here with coaching in mind."

Alex frowned. This was something he found difficult to understand. Why would anyone who had the education for coaching turn his back on it?

"You mean you changed your major?"

"I did more than that," Rick Preston told him.

"I changed my heart."

Alex stared at him. "You'll have to give that to me again. You've lost me somewhere."

"I was in my junior year when a guy about our age came to the campus and presented to me the claims Jesus Christ has on my life. After I gave my heart to the Lord, I saw that there was something more important to do than coaching; so I gave it up."

Alex's eyes glinted warily. "What is it you're doing now?"

"I suppose you could say that Karen and I are missionaries to the kids who go to Minnesota U."

"I see." Alex turned that over in his mind. He was

beginning to understand why Robin had invited their guests for that evening. He saw now why she had been so shaken up when he told her that he had to study.

"And I suppose you came here to convert me?" Anger tinged his voice.

"We couldn't convert anyone," Rick told him.

"The Holy Spirit has to do that."

"Who sent you here?"

"Nobody." Rick spoke with a frankness Alex could not miss. "We've been making routine calls and got to your name, that's all. And after we got acquainted with Robin, she asked us over for dinner. So here we are."

A definite chill settled over the conversation.

"I don't know what Robin told you about me," Alex spoke warningly, "and I don't care a lot, one way or the other. But I can tell you this much. You're wasting your time trying to stuff that religion down me. Robin has put some real experts on my trail, and none of them has nailed me yet. And what's more, they're not about to."

Sarcasm darkened his smile.

"So, if you're over here tonight with the idea of getting me 'saved,' you can just as well save your breath. I'm not buying it!"

Rick Preston's expression did not change. "I've never yet forced myself onto someone who didn't want to talk about spiritual things."

"That's good! Then you and I should get along fine."

A moment or two later Robin called dinner and the four of them sat around the table.

"Tell us something about your work," Robin said, glancing at Rick. "I've been so anxious to hear about it."

Alex glared at her.

"There's not much to tell," Rick said. "We go around and talk to people. Sometimes they listen and sometimes they don't."

Karen spoke up. "Why don't you tell Alex about the football player you talked with yesterday?"

Rick cast a warning glance at her. "I really don't think Alex would be interested."

"But I would," Robin countered.

Their guest told the story as briefly as possible and changed the subject.

Robin was disappointed in him. He didn't seem to act as though he cared whether he presented Christ to Alex or not. The evening didn't go at all as she had been hoping it would. Alex was pleasant enough to Rick when he talked about other things, but when Karen or Robin tried to steer the conversation to the things of God, he bristled noticeably. And when the guests finally left, nothing tangible had been accomplished. There hadn't even been an opportunity to witness to Alex, except for the brief mention of the sort of work Rick and Karen did.

A great weariness all but overwhelmed Robin as she said goodbye and closed the door. She turned back into the living room to see Alex facing her belligerently.

"Robin!" he exploded. "Suppose you tell me what was the big idea?"

"What do you mean?"

"Now, don't give me that stuff. You know very well what I mean. You staged this whole affair. You got them over here so they'd preach to me, didn't you?"

She did not answer.

"You don't have to tell me. I know you did it!" His voice raised in anger. "I've told you about this before, Robin, but I'm warning you again! Don't ever try anything like that another time! Don't you ever try to trap me into listening to that religion of yours again. Understand?"

A tear escaped Robin's eyelashes and trickled, unheeded, down her cheek.

"I–I thought it would be interesting to have Rick and Karen over for dinner," she stammered. "Since Rick had been interested in coaching too, I thought you would enjoy visiting with him."

"Yeah! Sure! That's the only reason you invited them over!" He turned away. "Don't make me laugh!"

When Alex went to his night watchman's job an hour later, Robin was lying on the bed, her shoulders twitching convulsively. Would Alex ever commit his life to Christ?

* * *

Although Doug played in every baseball game that season, he did little to establish himself in the eyes of the fans as a baseball player. He was batting a weak .209 and had made some costly fielding errors. It was only by the greatest good fortune that he had not cost Fairview a victory or two by his bumbling. Still, he dug in and played with such fervor that the coach kept him in. He was a spark plug to keep the others putting out their best.

On the way home from school after a game in which he had dropped two successive flies to allow a run to score, he was particularly discouraged.

"I don't know why the coach doesn't make me turn in my suit, Larry," he said. "I was miserable out there this afternoon."

"Anybody can have a little bad luck."

"It isn't bad luck when it happens as often as it does with me. I don't know why I can't play any better than I do."

In the final game of the junior high season against Foreston, Fairview got off to a shaky start. Larry Larson drew the pitching assignment but walked the first two batters and threw a home-run pitch to the next to put them behind 3-0. He got by well enough in the second and third innings, but in the fourth a little blooper fly over the second baseman's head started a rally that drove Larry out of the box with a five-hit, two-run barrage. With two out Doug speared a hard line drive to rob Foreston of a sure double and to retire the side.

After that Fairview seemed to come alive. They began to start chipping away at the Foreston lead, driving in one run in the fifth, three in the sixth, and another in the eighth to tie the score. When Doug came to bat with two down, there was a man on first.

Doug was trembling with excitement! He took the first pitch – a high, fast ball that just caught the corner for strike one. The next pitch was a ball. Doug started to swing but checked himself in time. A tense, expectant hush settled over the crowd. The game was riding on each pitch.

Doug stepped nervously out of the batter's box and wiped his palms on the sides of his trousers. He swung at the next pitch, catching a piece of it to pop a short fly foul into the stands just short of first base. He had to get a hit. He–.

The pitcher drew back and fired a fast ball through the middle. Doug swung savagely. The crash of the ball against the bat resounded through the stands like the report of a .22 rifle. He streaked for first. The man who had batted just ahead of him, and got on base by an error, scrambled around second and streaked for third.

The Foreston fielder came in fast, scooped the ball off the ground on the second hop and fired it home. But his throw was both wide and two yards short. The winning run came charging in.

Del, caught up in the excitement of the victory, was yelling the same as everyone else, at first. Then he stopped suddenly. That was the way it always was: let Doug get lucky and get a hit, and everybody went wild. He had never seen anyone so lucky.

* * *

DeeDee came into the living room where Danny Orlis was sitting. Seeing her, he put his paper aside.

"Hi, DeeDee."

Her lithe young body stiffened. She would have retorted coldly, but her voice caught. She shouldn't treat Danny the way she did. He only did what he did because he loved her and wanted to see her living a separated Christian life. When she considered the matter sensibly, that was the only conclusion she could come to. If her dad had lived, she knew that he would have insisted that she do most of the things Danny insisted on. Even when she was the angriest at him, she had to acknowledge that was true.

Shame stabbed through her as she eyed him sadly. For a brief moment she was filled with an impulse to go running over to him and tell him how sorry she was for the way she had treated him. But she did not move.

"Did you want something?" A certain tenderness crept into her voice.

"Not particularly. I just haven't seen you all day, that's all."

She went over and sat down across from him.

Danny asked her about her classes and wanted to know if she had brought home any grades lately.

She told him about an English theme she had to write. "I think I'll write about Del and his crow. We're supposed to write about something unusual. And I don't know of anything more unusual than the way Blackie follows Del around now that he doesn't keep him caged anymore."

Danny leaned back and crossed his legs.

"It makes me think of the crow I had when I was a boy. He used to sit on the trellis outside the back door and wait for me to come out. He'd fly along with me almost anywhere I went."

DeeDee let the conversation lapse. Once or twice she moistened her lips as though to speak, then changed her mind.

Danny noticed her indecision. "Is there something you'd like to talk with me about, DeeDee?"

Color rushed to her cheeks.

"Oh, no!" She quickly got to her feet. "Nothing special." She moved toward her bedroom. "I'd better go in and start studying. I've got loads of homework to do."

Danny watched as she disappeared from view, concern dulling his eyes. He still had not moved when Kay came up beside him.

"I saw that you were talking with DeeDee."

He nodded.

"I thought maybe she had started to open up to you, so I stayed in the kitchen."

His smile came and went.

"I thought she was going to. She even acted as though she wanted to, but she didn't really say anything."

"I'm sorry she didn't. DeeDee has been acting so strangely lately," Kay observed. "She seems to want to serve the Lord but is afraid of missing out on some fun."

They went back into the kitchen, and Danny sat at the table talking with his wife while she started dinner.

In her bedroom DeeDee spread her books before her on the desk and tried to study, but her mind kept going back to Danny and the way she had been treating him. There were times when she got so mad at him that she didn't think she could stand it another minute. But when she stopped to think about it, she had to admit that she wasn't being fair with him in acting as she did. Deep in her heart she knew that Danny and Kay loved her and the boys as much as their own parents had loved them, and that they were concerned that she have a good time.

Of course they didn't let her do the things Sandy's parents let her do, but that was because they didn't have the money to buy so much and because they were concerned that she and her brothers know the real, lasting happiness of dedicated Christian lives.

DeeDee closed her books and stared pensively at the wall. In a way she was glad that Danny and Kay wouldn't let her do everything she wanted to. It gave her a sense of security to know that they were watching and ready to stop her if she started doing things she shouldn't do as a Christian – things that could spoil her whole life. She knew she should go in and tell Danny how she felt.

With that in mind she got up and moved in the direction of the door. But, with her hand on the knob, she stopped.

If she apologized and told him exactly how she felt about it, he might ask her to quit running around with Sandy and Wally Crowder and the other kids. And she'd just die if she had to do that.

As she turned back, her uneasiness continued to grow. She was so confused! She really didn't know what she wanted. It was like being two persons at once, and neither one could agree with the other. At that moment DeeDee felt miserable.

CHAPTER 11

FURTHER AWAY THAN EVER

A severe depression caught Robin Smith in its icy, vicelike grip during the days that followed the dinner party to which she had invited the Prestons. She had been so sure that the visit of the campus workers had been of the Lord and that surely, this time, Alex was going to give his heart to Christ. She had even made herself believe it was possible that he would take a stand that very night, as soon as Rick began to talk with him. Instead, he had exploded with a violence that staggered her.

All day the Saturday following the dinner Robin debated whether or not to go to church. One minute she thought she would – that it would be a testimony to Alex if she went alone. The next she wondered what he would say if she did. It might just cause another big row, and she didn't think she could stand that. In the end she asked him if he cared if she went.

"Why should I care if you go to church?" he demanded petulantly. "It doesn't mean anything to me one way or the other, just as long as you don't try to drag me there."

Her lips quivered. "It–it would be nice to have you go with me. I haven't gotten to know anyone there yet. It's so much better if I don't have to go alone."

He frowned deeply. "I warned you, Robin. Don't start that again! I won't stand for it!"

"I just asked if you'd go with me so I wouldn't have to go alone."

"I heard what you asked me." There was a razor edge to his voice. "That's why I want to set things straight. I'm not going with you to church, so you'd just as well forget it."

It was all she could do to keep back the tears.

"If you don't want to go alone," Alex continued, belligerently, "don't go! Nobody's making you!"

She started to reply, hotly, but stopped. If she said anymore, Alex would get furious and they'd have another fight. She turned quickly so he couldn't see the hurt that flickered in her eyes.

She had been praying for Alex's salvation harder than she had ever prayed for anything in her life, but it didn't seem as though God was ever going to answer those prayers for her. Alex seemed more antagonistic to the gospel and further from making a decision for Christ than he had ever been. At least when they were first married, he would go to her church in Fairview with her once in a while. And if she agreed to go to his church, he would go without protesting. Now he seemed to have such hate in his heart for anything Christian that he wouldn't go anywhere and was so bitter and antagonistic that he got mad at the very mention of Christ.

The next morning Robin got up a little earlier than usual for Sunday morning and put on her best dress. Alex, who was lounging in an old robe, eyed her critically.

"Going somewhere?" he asked.

Their eyes met.

"I–I thought I'd go to church today."

Alex scowled. "After I've had to study all week and you've had to work at the store, I'd think the least you could do would be to stay home and spend the day with me."

Robin hesitated. She could read the danger signals in his taut voice.

"I–I won't be gone very long."

"Long enough to ruin the morning, that's all."

"Did, I mean, do you have anything special planned that you want to do?"

It was his turn to pause.

"I haven't had a chance to talk with you all week," he said lamely.

Briefly Robin's temper flared. He didn't actually want to talk to her, she knew. He just wanted to keep her from going to church. She didn't know why he had to be so stubborn and unreasonable. It was bad enough that he wouldn't go himself. Why did he have to keep hounding her to stay at home, too?

Anger glittered in her eyes, and she sat in silence at the breakfast table. But she didn't dare give voice to the way she felt. If she did, he would fly into a rage and stay mad for a week.

Alex dawdled over his coffee. She only briefly answered his clumsy attempts to draw her into conversation. A heavy silence fell over them. At last he could stand it no longer.

"What's the matter?"

No answer.

"What's the matter?" he demanded.

"If you don't know," she retorted bitterly, "I'm not going to tell you."

He reached out and captured her small hand in his own big fist.

"You aren't going to let *religion* cause trouble between us again, are you?"

Robin was trembling. There had been a time when doing what God wanted her to do had been more important to her than anything else in the world. Then she had turned her back on His call into full-time Christian service and married Alex. Now she couldn't even go to church without having a big argument.

What had happened to her?

* * *

The following Friday night DeeDee stayed with Sandy Cole.

"Wally said he was thinking about having a party tonight," Sandy explained when they were in her room alone. "But I guess things haven't worked out for him. He hasn't called or anything."

DeeDee breathed deeply. She was thankful Wally wasn't going to have a party. At least she wouldn't have to think up some excuse for not going.

"I'm glad of that." She spoke her mind without thinking.

Sandy eyed her quickly. "Just why did you say that?"

"I–I–." The other girl fumbled desperately for words. "I'd just rather be here with you. We always have so much fun when we come to your place."

DeeDee intended to pay her friend a compliment; but instead, a strange, hurt look gleamed in Sandy's eyes. Again that uneasiness had come back. There must be something terribly wrong in Sandy's life. Something she didn't want DeeDee or anyone else to know about.

"What's the matter, Sandy?" she asked, her voice soft and understanding.

Sandy straightened quickly. The mask slipped back into place and the hurt was hidden once more.

"There's nothing the matter. Why?"

"You looked so sad a moment ago."

Sandy's smile came and went, fleetingly.

"Oh, no. You're badly mistaken if you think I'm upset about something. There's nothing wrong and I'm not sad. In fact, I've never felt better in all my life." She got up and crossed the floor quickly. "To tell you the truth, DeeDee, I've got everything any girl could want, and this has been the very best year of my life."

DeeDee said no more to her about it, but it seemed to her that Sandy had protested too strongly. She acted as though she was trying to convince DeeDee of something. Something that she didn't actually believe herself.

The girls played records for a short period and finished their studies. They were just getting ready for bed when they heard a loud noise downstairs.

DeeDee jerked erect. "Wh-what was that?"

Sandy's thin face blanched. It was a moment or two before she spoke. "I–I don't think it was anything," she stammered weakly.

It came again – the sound of a heavy object falling.

"It is, too, something! Let's go down and see!"

She started for the door, but Sandy grabbed her by the arm.

"No! Please!" she pleaded. "Don't go down there!"

CHAPTER 12

THE COLES' SECRET

For the space of a minute or two, silence gripped DeeDee and Sandy in its icy grip. The two girls stared at each other, terror glinting in their eyes.

At last, DeeDee spoke, her desperation lacing her voice. "What is it, Sandy?" The words were little more than a whisper.

Her friend's lips parted as though to speak, but at that instant a blustering, slurred voice resounded through the house.

"Thelma!" the male voice cried. "Thelma! Where are you?"

The voice sounded strangely familiar to DeeDee, but there was a tone in it that was different than she had ever heard before.

"Is–is that your dad?"

Sandy nodded. She was biting her lower lip, and

DeeDee saw that she was having trouble keeping back tears.

DeeDee's eyes widened. Now she knew that Sandy's dad figured prominently in the sadness that reflected in her eyes. She had never been around anyone who had been drunk; but, instinctively, she knew that was the cause for his boisterous yelling.

"Thelma!" he cried again. "Get yourself down here and get me somethin' to eat. I'm hungry!"

The silence was deafening.

"You'd better get yourself down here and get me somethin' to eat, if you know wha's good for you! Thelma!"

He paused, waiting.

"Thelma! I know you're up there! Are you goin' to come down, or do I have to go up and drag you outa bed? It don' make no difference to me!"

He must have started for the stairs and stumbled over a piece of furniture. There was the sound of someone falling, followed by muffled cursing.

DeeDee studied her friend's ashen face. What should she say? What could she say?

The girls heard the bedroom door across the hall open and close. An instant later footsteps padded down the stairs.

"You sure took your own sweet time comin' down here!" he muttered. "Wha's the matter, Thelma? Ain't you glad t' see me?"

"Should I be glad to see you?" Her voice was icy.

"Come on, Thelma." His tone changed. "Gimme a little kiss t' show me you're glad I'm back."

Mrs. Cole's voice raised. "Stay away from me, Brad!" she exploded. "Don't you touch me!"

He must have stumbled towards her. DeeDee heard the sound of heavy footsteps again.

"Now, tha's no way to talk to your husban'. You're supposed to be a kin', loving wife. Remember?"

"How many times have I told you to stay away from me when you're so stinking, stumbling drunk?" Her voice was raised imperiously. "I don't know why you even want to come home when you're in that condition. If you don't care anything about me, think about Sandy. Do you want to ruin her life, too?"

It was almost a minute before either of them spoke again.

"Sure, I'm drunk," he blurted. "I admit it! I'm a no-good, drunken bum! But I've got reason t' drink, and don' you ever forget it! I've got plenty of reason t' drink!"

Mrs. Cole ignored his accusation.

"I don't know why I put up with this, Brad!" There was a thin, high-pitched whine to her voice. "I don't know why I put up with it. Any other woman would have left you a long time ago, and you know it."

"There y' go!" he blurted. "Nag. Nag. Nag. That's all I ever hear around home! Do this. Don't do this. Get me something else! I don' like that! Y' wanna know why I drink so much? It's to get away from your naggin'. That's why!"

By this time, he was shouting so the neighbors next door could hear him.

"Brad!" Mrs. Cole broke in sharply. "Sandy has a girlfriend upstairs!" Her voice lowered as she continued. "We don't want them to hear us! We don't want everyone in town to know what a miserable drunk you are!"

Instantly his voice softened until all that the girls could hear were the muffled sounds of voices downstairs. DeeDee and Sandy stared at each other, shocked to silence by the episode they had just heard. At last DeeDee was able to speak once more.

"Oh, Sandy," she whispered. "I'm so terribly sorry for you!"

It was all the other girl could do to choke back the sobs that were welling up inside of her. Her voice quavered. "I–I didn't want you to know!" Yet, her expression relaxed as though she was glad, somehow, that DeeDee was aware of the problem.

DeeDee put her arm about her friend's shoulder, comfortingly. "I'm so sorry!"

Sandy jerked erect, wiping away her tears. A fierce loyalty firmed the lines in her young face. "Daddy isn't really like that!" she blurted. "When–when he's himself, he's the grandest person you would ever want to know. He's so kind and sweet and generous and–."

It was as though the effort of speaking had expended her energy and she was unable to say anything else.

DeeDee continued to look at her. In that moment she saw her friend in an entirely new light. She had always been so envious of the things Sandy had and the way Sandy and her parents lived. Now she saw that her best friend really had nothing at all. Her home life was miserable, and all the clothes and 'things' she had couldn't make up for all her unhappiness. They were only a shell that she used to cover the emptiness in her life.

It was some time before Sandy spoke again. And when she did, bitterness made her voice harsh and ugly.

"There are times when I think I can't stand living the way we have to," she said. "I feel like running away so far that I wouldn't even be able to find out how to get back to Fairview."

It frightened DeeDee to hear her friend talk that way. "Running off wouldn't do any good. It would only make things worse."

Now that Sandy began to talk, the words tumbled out, one upon another.

"You can say that because you don't know what it's like to live in the kind of a house I have to live in. I don't care what you say, DeeDee. I can't keep on staying here and listening to them fight the way they do." She reached out impulsively and grasped DeeDee's arm. "Do you know, there are times when

Mother won't speak to Daddy for two or three weeks in a row? And before she'll make up with him, he has to buy her something like new furniture or an expensive dress or–or something new for me."

DeeDee said nothing. That explained the huge wardrobe of new dresses Sandy had and the reason Mrs. Cole was so free in lending one to DeeDee.

After a time, Sandy continued. "But even that doesn't help very long. Daddy goes out to the club and gets to gambling or drinking, and it starts all over again. The trouble is that they don't love each other anymore. They don't even love me!"

She made no attempt to turn away this time to hide the tears.

"Of course they love you, Sandy," DeeDee replied. "And I'm sure they love each other, too."

Sandy shook her head. "If they really loved me, they wouldn't do the things they do."

She began to cry so hard that she wasn't able to go on talking.

DeeDee was silent as her friend sobbed heart-brokenly. She wanted to tell her how the Lord Jesus could help her and her parents, but she could not find the words to begin, words that would explain God's love for them. If only she had talked more to Sandy about the Lord, she thought ruefully, she wouldn't feel so awkward and speechless now.

Finally, after Sandy quit crying, DeeDee tried to talk with her about other things but was only successful in changing the subject for a few moments. Then Sandy did not want to talk about anything. Neither of the girls slept much that night.

The next morning when Sandy and DeeDee got up, Mr. Cole's car was still in the driveway, but he was nowhere in sight. DeeDee supposed he was in one of the upstairs bedrooms sleeping, but she didn't dare to ask. Mrs. Cole was in the kitchen fixing breakfast when they came down.

She looked up, smiling with forced brightness.

"Hello, girls, I didn't expect you to be up quite so early this morning."

"We have things to do," Sandy said shortly.

"Did you sleep well?"

Sandy kept her eyes averted so she was not looking directly into her mother's face. "I guess so."

DeeDee said nothing at all. The only thing she could see was the dark half-circle under Mrs. Cole's left eye. The woman had tried to hide it with powder or some kind of make-up, but it showed through, a livid blue-black. DeeDee didn't think she was staring, but Sandy's mother saw that she was looking at it.

"I see that you're wondering what happened to me last night," she said, managing a sheepish little laugh, as though it was nothing at all.

DeeDee felt her cheeks color with embarrassment. "I–I–."

"Don't feel badly about it. If I saw you with an eye as puffed and black and swollen as this one, I'd be wondering what happened, too." She was busy putting the plates and silver on the table. "You can believe it or not, but I stumbled and fell against the dresser last night. I hit the sharp corner of the dresser top. It's a wonder I didn't split it open and have to have some stitches taken."

There was quiet desperation in her voice, as though she was anxious to have DeeDee say something that would indicate she believed the made-up story.

"That's too bad," the girl mumbled.

DeeDee was sure that wasn't the way Mrs. Cole got the black eye, but she had to go along with it. Her gaze met Sandy's. She could tell by the look on her friend's face that she didn't believe her mother's story, either. But there was something else in Sandy's eyes – a gratitude that DeeDee had not blurted out her own disbelief.

* * *

DeeDee thought about letting Danny and Kay Orlis know what had happened at the Cole home the night before when she was staying there. If she did, she reasoned, maybe they would pray for them. It might even be that she could convince Danny that it would do some good if he would seek out Mr. Cole and talk with him about his need to become a Christian, so he could quit drinking and change the terrible way he was living. Once or twice she was ready to tell the Orlises about it but at the last instant decided against it.

Danny and Kay were so opposed to drinking and that sort of thing that they might never let her go back to Sandy's for a night, or even an evening, if they found out what Mr. Cole was actually like.

Somehow, since DeeDee found out about the trouble at the Cole home, it seemed to her that Sandy was even closer to her than before. Sandy acted as though she had to have someone to talk to. Someone who wouldn't laugh at her or tell the things she shared. She had never revealed any of her problems to DeeDee before, but now she shared everything with her. She confided all her hopes and fears to DeeDee and even seemed pleased when DeeDee volunteered to pray for her mother and dad.

"Do you think it would help any?" Sandy asked. The thin edge of doubt honed her voice.

"I *know* that God answers prayer," DeeDee told her.

Sandy smiled gratefully. "You used to say that I was the best friend you ever had, but now I can say that you're the best friend I ever had."

"I'm only glad I can do something to help," DeeDee said, sighing. "It doesn't seem that there's very much I can do. I can't go and talk with them or anything."

"Just having someone to talk to helps a lot."

DeeDee smiled. It wasn't that she was glad Sandy's parents were having trouble. She'd give *anything* if they would both accept Christ as their Savior and get all their troubles straightened out. But it was good to know that Sandy needed her – that she was able to help her in some small way. She was glad that Sandy thought enough of her as a friend to confide in her and to ask her to pray.

DeeDee could scarcely dare to hope so much, but maybe Sandy would make a decision for Christ too. Then she would have a *Christian* friend! She began to pray for Sandy, as well as Mr. and Mrs. Cole, asking God to help all three of them to make decisions for Him.

At the supper table that night when it came time for their evening devotions, DeeDee had an unspoken prayer request. Del and Doug eyed her curiously.

"What's that all about?" Doug blurted.

"Doug!" Danny faced him sternly. "You know that is something we never ask about. If we have someone with an unspoken prayer request, we honor it without asking any questions."

"I'm sorry. It just popped out."

"The prayer request isn't for me," DeeDee continued, grateful for Danny's intervention. "It's for someone else, but I–I can't say anything more than that."

"You don't have to explain," Danny told her. "If anyone has a prayer request he wishes to remain unspoken, that's fine. We won't ask any questions."

Usually only one person prayed for a specific request, but that night everyone prayed for DeeDee's unspoken request. It seemed that there was such an urgency in her voice.

* * *

It was almost a week later when DeeDee met Sandy on the streets of Fairview. She had seen her every day at school, of course. But this time Sandy acted as though something extremely important had just happened. Her eyes were sparkling and the smile she wore was more relaxed and happy than DeeDee had seen in a long, long while.

"Hi, DeeDee!" Her entire being seemed to light up.

"What is it, Sandy?" She grasped her friend by the arm. "What happened?"

"You'll never be able to guess!"

DeeDee's spirits soared. "Is it your parents?"

Sandy nodded. "I was going to have Mom take me out to your place this evening so I could tell you about it. I'm so happy I just about cry whenever I think about it!"

They started down the street together. Sandy didn't speak immediately, and DeeDee waited with growing impatience. Mr. and Mrs. Cole must have made decisions for Christ and got all their differences worked out for Sandy to be so happy as she seemed to be. Finally, Sandy stopped and, looking about to see that no one was close, she turned to face DeeDee.

"You–you remember that–that terrible thing that

happened the night you were staying over at our place, don't you?" she began.

DeeDee nodded. How could she forget? She had never heard anything so terrible. "I've been praying about your parents every night since then," she replied.

"And I want to thank you for that. That was the main reason I wanted to come out and–and tell you about Mother and Daddy."

"What happened?"

"Well," Sandy went on, "for a while Mother wouldn't speak to Daddy again, and I thought it was going to be just like all the other times when he'd have to buy her something expensive to get her to be nice to him again. But that wasn't the way it was! *This time it was different!*"

"You mean–," DeeDee gasped. Even though she had been praying and hoping that things would change at the Cole house, she found it difficult to believe Mr. and Mrs. Cole would ever quit their quarreling and fighting.

"Daddy and Mother finally got together and had a long talk about the–the way they've been living and the things they've been doing. They finally decided that they couldn't go on the way they've been doing."

"That's wonderful!" DeeDee breathed.

"They're going to quit going to those parties out at the country club, for one thing. And Daddy promised that he isn't going to drink anymore. He isn't even going to take a social drink with his old friends. And DeeDee, ever since that night he hasn't touched a drop. Isn't that marvelous?"

Tears welled up in DeeDee's eyes. "I'm so happy for you," she said. "I'm so happy for all of you."

"It's been just wonderful around the house since–since Mother and Daddy decided to change," Sandy went on. "You wouldn't know how different it is now."

Sandy wiped at her eyes, too.

"I have to keep pinching myself to know that it's real. It seems like some sort of heavenly dream or something."

"I can imagine how you feel, Sandy. I–I'll keep on praying for them."

Her friend shrugged slightly. "That probably helps," she acknowledged, "and I do appreciate your praying for them. But it's like Daddy says. Two intelligent, sensible people should be able to get together and patch up their differences without all the sort of trouble they have been having. He says a man can quit drinking if he just wants to badly enough."

As they separated, DeeDee was still glowing with the wonderful news that Brad and Thelma Cole had been able to talk things out and were going to change their lives. She knew how excited and relieved Sandy must be to have them happy instead of fighting. And DeeDee was happy just to know that her friend was happy now.

Yet, something about the matter disturbed DeeDee. She couldn't help thinking about what Sandy has said, especially about a sensible, intelligent couple patching up their differences. She felt a distinct disappointment and wished that God would figure a little more in their plans. It would be a lot easier for them to make the changes they knew had to be made in their lives.

When DeeDee got back to the Orlis home, Danny had just come in from the airport.

"Say, now," he exclaimed. "You look happy this afternoon."

"I am," replied DeeDee with a smile.

Although her smile faded, the glow in her eyes remained. She looked about, thoughtfully. There had been so many times since she started running with Sandy when she had been jealous of all the things her friend had. She had been resentful because Danny didn't have the money to buy the same kind of clothes for her and have the same kind of a house and the same expensive furniture.

Now she realized anew how much more Danny and Kay were giving her. How much joy and happiness a consistent Christian testimony meant! She was seeing how little real enjoyment came from the things the Coles had, and how their indifference to the things Sandy did was because they were so selfish, so wrapped up in their own problems. Danny and Kay didn't let her and the boys do whatever they wanted to, because they were concerned, because they loved them and were anxious that they grow up to be consistent Christians.

She would keep on praying for the Coles, she decided firmly. And for Sandy, too. And she would be more faithful in witnessing to her.

Her smile came back once more, tenderly. She went over to Danny, put her arms about his neck and kissed him lightly on the cheek.

He stared at her.

"What was that for?" he asked, a half grin lifting one corner of his mouth.

"Just for being 'you,' " she said, mysteriously, and swept into her bedroom.

He stared after her, scratching his head.

"What's the matter?" Kay asked him quietly.

"Search me. But I can tell you one thing. I sure can't understand girls."

"You're not supposed to," Kay told him playfully.

THE DANNY ORLIS SERIES

The Danny Orlis series, by Bernard Palmer, delivers a blend of adventure, mystery, and suspense through various settings—from the Canadian wilderness to Guatemalan jungles. Danny Orlis, an adept outdoorsman, skilled athlete, and committed Christian, employs his quick thinking, calm bravery, and biblical solutions to confront everyday problems and hair-raising dangers. Early stories focus on Danny navigating school life, sports, and outdoor challenges, while in later books, Danny and his wife Kay provide wisdom and guidance to youngsters facing lifelike situations and challenges. Having sold over two million copies, this series has made Palmer a renowned author in Christian youth literature. Palmer is also the author of the Felicia Cartright series and various other series for Christian youth.

AVAILABLE FROM WWW.ANEKOPRESS.COM